T0365247

THE
CHANGING
OF THE
GODS

ANTHONY MIANO

authorHOUSE·

AuthorHouse™
1663 Liberty Drive
Bloomington, IN 47403
www.authorhouse.com
Phone: 833-262-8899

Published by AuthorHouse 01/04/2022

ISBN: 978-1-6655-4757-4 (sc)
ISBN: 978-1-6655-4762-8 (e)

Print information available on the last page.

This book is printed on acid-free paper.

Because of the dynamic nature of the Internet, any web addresses or links contained in
this book may have changed since publication and may no longer be valid. The views
expressed in this work are solely those of the author and do not necessarily reflect the
views of the publisher, and the publisher hereby disclaims any responsibility for them.

CONTENTS

DISCLAIMERS

TRIGGER WARNING: The following story contains frank discussions of war, Post Traumatic Stress, violence, child murder, adultery, sexual assault and religion. Reader discretion is advised.

ACKNOWLEDGMENTS

The authors of the stories that provided the jumping off points for my story: Euripedes (The Trojan Women) and Homer (The Iliad and The Odyssey).

Michael Fontaine, Professor of Classics, Cornell University. After seeing him on the History Channel series Clash of the Gods I sent him my notes for the initial story concept. He encouraged me to proceed with writing it out.

Editor Megan Sanders, whose professional expertise helped transform my semi-literate scrawl into something publishable.

The Ohio Media School, for providing me with the network and platform to promote this story, and Katherine Miracle in particular. Before enrolling in her Media Sales and Marketing Emphasis program I had written the first and last chapters. The Emphasis program gave me the push to write out the rest.

The United States Army, Army National Guard and Army Reserve, for helping me gain the perspective of a soldier.

My parents Ann Besch, Thomas Besch and Joe Miano for putting up with me for the last 30+ years and giving me much of the military perspective that went into this story.

LIST OF CHARACTERS

Hades- God of the Underworld.

Zeus- King of the Olympians.

Poseidon- God of the Sea.

Hera- Queen of the gods.

Athena-Goddess of wisdom and strategy.

Ares-God of war.

Apollo- God of the sun, twin brother of Artemis.

Artemis- Goddess of the hunt, twin sister of Apollo.

Hermes- Messenger of the gods.

Hephaestus- God of the forge.

Aphrodite- Goddess of love and beauty.

Dionysus-God of wine and celebration.

Hercules-Demigod, son of Zeus.

Hector- Fallen prince of Troy.

Persephone- Wife of Hades, queen of the Underworld.

Odysseus-King of Ithaca, creator of the Trojan Horse.

Charon- Boatman who transported the dead to the Underworld.

Priam- Fallen king of Troy.

Agamemnon- King of Mycenae, commanding general of Greeks during Trojan War.

Iphigenia-Daughter of Agamemnon, sacrificed for the wind to get to Troy.

Medusa-Former priestess of Athena, converted into a monster as punishment for being raped.

Tiresias-Blind prophet, resident of the Underworld. Sees more than those who have sight.

Cerberus- Three headed guard dog of the Underworld, tasked with keeping the dead inside.

CHAPTER ONE

FALL OF TROY

"Only the dead have seen the end of war."
-Plato, ancient Greek philosopher
and founder of the Academy

T rojan women. Trojan children. Trojans of all ages and a few Greek soldiers. As the marauding Greek army slashed, stabbed, and torched its way through the once impenetrable interior of the great city, all those who perished that night filed into the Underworld in great numbers. Hades observed them all with a mixture of resignation, disgust, pity, and anger. The meddling of his brothers and sisters in mortal affairs resulted in the most significant mass immigration he had ever received.

The god of the Underworld was the final authority to reign over every human who had ever lived. He had seen new arrivals killed in horrible ways before: turned to stone, cooked to death in a hollow statue called the Brazen Bull, ripped apart by the Minotaur, eaten by a cyclops, but those were the actions of individuals. The influx of new residents this night was the culmination of years of scheming and manipulation by the almighty pantheon.

At the end of the long line of Trojans stood the recently deposed King Priam. The sight of a monarch arriving was the most frequent indicator of the end of a war in the mortal world. As Hades approached, Priam's face bore the speechless expression of a man whose world had been destroyed and family slaughtered.

"Priam, don't look surprised. You always knew you'd meet me one day."

"Yes, I did always know. However, I always thought I would arrive alone. My subjects were not supposed to join me. My *sons* were supposed to bury *me*."

"You are not the first father to bury his sons, your majesty. You will be far from the last. I feel I must apologize. If my brothers and sisters had to face the consequences for *anything* they had ever done, it would not have gone this far."

"As soon as Helen entered my walls, this became inevitable."

"No, it did not. It became unavoidable one step at a time. Some steps were bigger than others. It occurs to me now that you and Agamemnon are inverses of each other. Iphigenia, come meet our newest resident."

She appeared instantaneously at Hades' request. Having resided in the Underworld for the last decade of mortal time (not that she was aware of it), the late daughter of Agamemnon appeared blank. The anger and resentment she left the mortal world with had devolved into nothing at all. Residing in the land of the dead had a way of purging human emotion and feeling. Priam saw the gash across Iphigenia's neck.

"You...were not killed in the war. How did you get here? You're too young."

"My father sacrificed me to Artemis to gain the wind to travel to Troy," she said with the same tone that she might have recounted her morning routine when she was alive. Priam's jaw plummeted like Icarus.

"Artemis? Is she not the protector of women? And why...? She has no interest in warfare!"

"Father killed a prized animal of hers. In his arrogance, he proclaimed himself her equal in hunting. Such an affront had to be punished." Iphigenia turned and rejoined the shuffling masses of Hades' domain.

This revelation shocked and disturbed Priam. He looked at Hades with disbelief. "I... watched Achilles drag my son's remains behind his chariot for days and yet that cruelty pales in comparison to what I have just heard. Hector was at least grown. He was a warrior who fought, bled, and died for his country. Anyone who falls by the blade should at least be holding one!"

"Yes, you protected your son Paris even after he provoked a war. Agamemnon killed an innocent child to escalate it. My niece could have stopped the madness right there. Yet the mortals will honor her as they do Zeus."

"I know you are a god but…how do you know?" Priam asked.

"The Fates sometimes speak to me. They speak to all of us Olympians sometimes. They have informed me that she will be honored with a grand temple. It will have marble columns gilded with gold and silver, works by renowned sculptors, and a massive statue of Artemis in the center. A monument to a goddess who demanded the blood of a child as a price to pay for the opportunity to spill *more* blood. *And* it will one day be declared one of humanity's greatest building achievements."

"We humans do have that inclination… to exalt those who kill and destroy."

"The Fates also tell me that the key players of the madness that engulfed Troy will also be worshipped. Mainly Achilles: your son was merely one of his many victims. Throw a stone here and you'll hit someone he killed. He will be held up as an example for men to emulate for centuries to come."

"How? Why?"

"I may as well share the story with you, Priam. Achilles was told early on he had to make a choice between a long, ordinary, and happy life where he would be forgotten soon after or a short, glorious one ending in battle and remembered as long as men walk the earth."

"I suppose I should take comfort in knowing that, by extension, so will Hector. I'm sure that battle will be written about and preserved for eternity in the collective human memory. I haven't seen Hecuba or Cassandra. Or Andromache. I think I know why."

"Yes, they have been spared, depending on one's perspective. All three have much more hardship ahead of them before they get here. I don't need the Fates to help me predict that. I am so sorry for everything, Priam."

"Your sentiment is appreciated but useless. It will not restore anything your victims have lost."

"*My* victims? My dear king, you assume because you and most of your subjects are in my domain that I brought you here. Tell me, did your priests even once communicate anything to you from *me*?"

"No, I don't believe they did."

"Exactly. Have you not ensured friends and relatives of yours would make it here after death, before the war?"

"Trojans practiced similar funeral rites as the Greeks for generations."

"So, your people always came here then. It happened even when we gods paid no attention to you. I ask you, what would I, the god of the dead, have to gain?"

"There is no incentive to make effort to acquire that which you would eventually gain anyway."

"That is an understatement, Priam. I have never seen mortals arrive here in such numbers. I'm not sure how long I can contain them here. The Fates say I might have an even larger pool to draw them from some day."

"I never thought I'd relate to any of the gods, Hades. Especially you. It appears though that you and I are bonded by a shared struggle. No one knows the difficulties our stations impose upon us."

"You are most correct. It doesn't take the wisdom of Athena to figure that one out. I rather think you had the better deal. Oh yes, I am powerful, but despised at worst, tolerated at best."

"You think I was unanimously loved?"

"Of course not. As you mortals often say, 'heavy is the head that wears the crown.' But you still presided over one of the richest and most beautiful kingdoms in human history. For centuries, Troy was a glittering jewel coveted by all men."

"A glittering jewel defended by rough men. Legendary places must, by necessity, breed legendary men to defend them. I raised Hector from birth to follow in my footsteps. I may be biased, of course, but I believed him to be the ideal man. Ready and willing to fight, bleed, kill and die for Troy but never eager to do so. He was haunted by his memories of the men he killed in battle, but I assured him it was a good thing. Royalty who has seen the horrors of war is far more careful about starting it."

"Ares tells me they will one day be the minority. I have seen the horrors of war too, Priam. My brothers and sisters and I fought one to overthrow our predecessors, the Titans, once. It was different for us though, being immortal. Immortality is a double-edged sword. Picture the most painful ways to die you can think of. Then, imagine surviving those ways and remembering *all of it.*"

"I had to see most of my other children die too Hades. I watched

Hecuba present a brave face to our people and that helped me do the same, but it destroyed a piece of me each time. She might not be here yet, but her heart has been for years. You gods with your eternal life spans can't begin to fathom this. You've never lost a child, you, Zeus, Poseidon, any of them."

"You're partially correct there. The combined children of us Olympians could form a sizable invasion force. We have watched them die before. In the case of some of them, we can't possibly lose them. Athena, Ares, Apollo and Artemis are all children of Zeus—I think. My brothers and sisters do get around. However, most of their offspring are demigods: half human, half divine. They have most of the strengths of gods, but they can still be killed. Hercules and Achilles are the only ones I can recall dying, and Hercules was promoted to full god by Zeus. If more of the demigods died, I don't think either of my brothers would shed a tear. Why would they when they have so many more?"

"I envy them. The worst part of seeing so many of my children die was the desperate hope, *every single time,* that it would be the last one. My wife and I *never* got desensitized to it, Hades. Damn you, *they* were supposed to bury US!"

Priam collapsed to the ground as though the bones had been removed from his legs. He cried so loud and so hard that for the first time ever, someone in the Underworld was heard on Earth. The fallen ruler did not die in ignorance. The Greeks did not kill him like an assassin prowling in the darkness. He had seen his beloved city in flames but did not live long enough to process its loss. Reflecting on that *and* the loss of his children simultaneously overwhelmed him completely.

Hades had never been the cruel and callous god he was believed to be. Mortals spoke of him in hushed tones, and many wouldn't even speak his name. The best thing most humans could say about him was, "Yes, he abducted his wife, but that was one bad deed measured against many more from Zeus and Poseidon." Some acknowledged that he did an unpleasant job that needed to be done, but most did not.

The cumulative tears of King Priam nearly formed a new river. Priam looked around at all his new neighbors. He considered gathering some Trojans to attack the few Greeks who had accompanied them here, but the fire inside was just gone. Despite all his best efforts, the kingdom of Troy had been relocated to the Underworld.

5

"What was it all for, Hades? What is the point of anything men do if *this* is the end of our journey?"

"Priam, I wonder that also. Oh, I know all about the abduction of Helen by the Trojan Prince Paris but, I still ask why. How can a man's desire of a woman justify all this? I might ask them directly. Did a Trojan farmer deserve to die for the failed marriage of a Greek king?"

"That was likely only the straw that broke the camel's back, Hades. Troy had been to war many times, never close to home soil. Our walls alone deterred all our previous enemies from mounting invasions. It was no secret that Agamemnon had lusted after Troy for many years and the abduction of Helen was just an excuse. He would have eventually found or created one anyway."

"So, it wasn't just a father's desire to see his son happy that made you reject the ultimatum to return her or face the combined wrath of all the Greeks?"

"Of course not. Don't misunderstand—it pleased me immensely to see Paris so happy. I knew Agamemnon could not be trusted. He would not have called off the invasion if I'd sent Helen back. I know it sounds like a simple matter of cold calculus—one life measured against many—but... if a leader becomes comfortable sacrificing one, soon he will comfortably sacrifice two. Then eventually, he has no limit. I'd guided Troy through several wars before. Affairs of state also weigh heavy in peace. I made decisions that sent my countrymen to their deaths so many times. The *only* thing that made me able to live with it was that I did it so Troy could endure."

"I am sorry, Priam. You are now free of that burden you carried for so many years. This series of unfortunate events has made me question the arrangements in place here. The children of Troy are now either here or awaiting delivery into bondage. It feels cruel to make them spend eternity in the same place as the men who stole their lives away from them."

"What could you possibly do with them otherwise?"

"I am considering a new organization, based on the conduct of the deceased. Right now, the only way anyone gets an afterlife different from what you see before us is to either gravely offend one of the gods or be a great hero—Tartarus, or the Elysian Fields. I think now a great many more mortals will go these places."

"And you will apply this to all mortals?"

"Of course, from the mightiest king to the lowliest peasant."

"If that is so, then what will you do with me?"

"I'm leaning more towards the Elysian Fields for you. Though you are certain otherwise, we will never know whether returning Helen to the Spartan king, Menelaus, would have prevented the war. I am inclined to punish you severely for your failure to stop it. On the other hand, you were a wise, kind, and just king for many years. I've welcomed in many rulers here before you. So many of them cared for nothing but themselves in life. They used their position only to indulge their appetites for gold, treasure, wealth, war, bloodshed, and carnal pleasures of all kinds. They saw the throne as their birthright. You, however, viewed it as something a king must live up to and not something he hides behind. Your regard for human life is unrivaled by any of your contemporaries. Most other royals feel no sorrow for the shortened lives of their subjects. Priam, if more mortal men were like you then *I* would have fewer subjects. You may enter paradise right now if you like."

"Not without Hecuba. All my wealth and power would have been meaningless without her. And I will not exalt myself even further above my people."

"Very well. I'm inclined to allow most of your people to join you though."

"Most?"

"I will have to evaluate their behavior in life as I have yours. Killers, rapists, thieves, abusers, and other evil doers will not get a pass just because they were cut down by Greek swords."

"Of course. Not all Trojans were noble and virtuous."

"Remember, you may have to wait for a while before all of your family can follow you. Besides Hecuba, I know for certain your son's wife and child still live. They will be carried off to Greek lands tomorrow. Your grandson, Astyanax, is quite young. He has a long life ahead of him."

CHAPTER TWO

BREAKING POINT

"In peace, sons bury their fathers. In war, fathers bury their sons."
-Herodotus, ancient Greek writer,
geographer, and historian

Hades sat in his gleaming black throne, flanked by his loyal companion, Cerberus. The hound napped, oblivious to his master's plight. His siblings' behavior had taken a toll on him for untold years. He had found it too pointless to intervene as, no matter his actions, all mortals would end up in his charge, eventually. However, the now concluded war pushed him to a limit he never knew he had.

Persephone entered the throne room, her face bearing an expression nearly as severe as his. Hades' mood usually improved when he saw his wife, but her stern look made this time an exception. Before he could even ask why, he saw the small, bloody, and mangled child she carried. His spirit filled with a rage that was normally reserved for his two oldest brothers.

"Hades, this is Astyanax. No, his remains weren't uncovered after the fall of Troy. He was killed afterwards."

"WHO DID THIS? If he's with me already, I'll feed pieces of him to Cerberus!"

"None of the men responsible are here yet, my love. Odysseus of Ithaca convinced his fellow Greek kings that the last son of Hector, the late prince of Troy, was too dangerous to be left alive. While powerless then, of course, they believed he would one day seek revenge. His rather unique appearance in death was due to being thrown from the city walls."

"Odysseus, the warrior king, best known for his *wisdom*? Using it to think his way out of problems, sure, but *this*? ATHENA, HOW CAN YOU FAVOR SUCH A MONSTER? Find Hephaestus; tell him to invent for me something like the Brazen Bull, only worse! I want it ready for when he gets here!"

Hades' outrage at Athena was intense enough to cause several small earthquakes.

"Hephaestus will have plenty of time. Hermes stopped by with an update. Apparently, the great Odysseus offended your sea dwelling brother by blinding one of his illegitimate children. He's ordered that Odysseus not be killed, for a while."

"I cannot turn back time. I cannot return the boy to life. However, I can facilitate justice. Hector of Troy, I summon thee!"

The late Prince Hector appeared in the throne room instantaneously. Although consumed by the general apathy of most of the dead, he retained most of his appearance and bearing he carried in life. A great man like him would take longer in the afterlife to forget who he was. Something in him reminded him he had been the great defender of Troy, even after learning of its demise. However, at the sight of his son, his mortal spirit was reactivated as strong as ever.

"Astyanax! I've missed you! I said goodbye to your mother before I faced Achilles, knowing you'd never... I don't have my helmet on; you know who I am, don't you?"

This newfound enthusiasm was replaced with confusion, despair, and rage once Astyanax's mangled appearance dawned on him. It suddenly occurred to him *why* he was seeing his son again so soon.

"I knew the Greeks would be merciless, but *this*? Was vanquishing me not enough to satisfy Achilles' lust for blood? I killed one of his family, so he had to kill one of mine? How could he even have known which child...?"

Hades placed his hand on the prince's shoulder to gently silence him.

"This was not the action of Achilles, Hector. Achilles has been here a few years now. Your son arrived only today."

9

Hades then took the child from his wife's arms and touched his hands to him. The blood and dirt washed away, and the broken bones reset. While this did not restore him, it would at least allow Hector to look at him as he appeared in life. Hector showed both elation and anger that Hades seldom saw on the faces of the dead.

"Odysseus will not be joining us here for some time. He has angered Poseidon and thus guaranteed himself a minimum of ten more years alive. My brother could kill him immediately but would rather he suffer. Once he has returned to Ithaca, my brother's protection will cease, and justice will be served. In the meantime, we shall help you prepare."

"How?"

"I will have Hephaestus craft you a new set of armor and weapons. The last thing you saw in life was some of his previous work—Achilles' armor. You'll have a new set just like it, except more *you*."

"What do you want in exchange?"

"I would say justice, but, since you're offering, I wonder if you could help me understand. *Why* did you face Achilles alone? Ares was baffled by your decision and he's the god of war. He said you had many other options available."

"Honor. Integrity. Bravery."

Hades' facial expression conveyed that he was both confused and intrigued.

"I wasn't just a playboy prince. I was also a warrior and leader of men. Facing him was the lesser evil."

"Lesser than what?"

"I needed to maintain the respect of my soldiers. Oh, they might have logically understood why, if I'd acted differently, but I wouldn't have the same loyalty anymore. A leader should never demand anything of his people that he wouldn't do himself. I could not in good conscience send men to their deaths when I wouldn't be willing to face it myself. What other options did Achilles tell you I could have chosen from?"

"You maintained archers on the walls at all times. I understand Achilles was later killed by an arrow anyway."

"Yes, he was. I could have ordered my archers to open fire on Achilles at the first opportunity. They likely would have killed him. That would have caused more problems though. Had I broken my word, it would have destroyed any chance that might have remained to stop the bloodshed. We would have had no chance left of negotiating an end to hostilities."

"You put the needs of your country ahead of your own. Most men in power wouldn't. I'd have fewer people here if they did."

"There was one more reason. I knew either outcome of my duel with Achilles would help stop him."

"I don't understand. How did your death help stop him?"

"Achilles was already the deadliest warrior in history. When I killed his cousin (or lover, reports vary) in battle, he became something else. We thought Ares himself was using him as an instrument. One of my advisors suggested we think up a way to *drop the walls of Troy on him*. We were grateful he never got the idea to penetrate the walls by himself—he was angry enough he might have succeeded. Killing me must have sated his extra blood lust. He was brought back down to his previous levels of proficiency after that."

"That's why you were willing to leave your wife widowed and your son fatherless?"

"I knew they would be cared for. You've seen my wife. She would have easily found another husband. Everyone saw me say good-bye to her and my son. What they didn't see was how I said good-bye to my brother."

"Paris?"

"Yes, I had several brothers, but for some reason most people will only know of *him*."

"Probably because of his role in starting the war."

"Yes, most likely because of that. I confronted him before I met Achilles. I politely asked him to take care of Astyanax should I not return."

"Politely?"

"Alright, I *ordered him* to care for my son after my certain death. I placed one hand over his throat and pinned him against the wall to emphasize my point. I told him that I agreed with father's decision not to turn him over to the Greeks, not out of brotherly love but out of patriotic duty. I told him that if our father and I had thought for even a second that his death would satisfy the Greek demand for vengeance, that I would have personally delivered his head to Menelaus."

"I will add Paris to my list."

"List?"

"The list of men and gods I intend to confront about their actions in the war. In some cases, their actions before the war too. Would you care to be present when I force Paris to explain himself?"

"Sure, but he already has."

"To you, yes. I mean for him to explain himself to *me*. I'm getting the idea that he doesn't deserve to have death wipe all the blood from his hands, and the innocents that died because of his lust do not deserve to spend eternity near him."

"I agree, my lord. I think he deserves more consequences than death. How can something that was inevitable regardless be sufficient punishment?"

"You're as wise as your father, Hector. Now, while Hephaestus *will* forge you a new set of weapons and armor, he can't forge your fighting skills for you. I suggest you begin preparing for your eventual confrontation with Odysseus. You probably won't feel it passing, not down here, but you have at least ten years to train."

"I look forward to it."

CHAPTER THREE

HEPHAESTUS, APHRODITE AND ARES

"Adultery is not a crime, it's an amusement."

-Kathleen Winsor, American author

L aden with a heavy pack full of iron ore, Hephaestus, the forger of the gods made his way into his workshop within his palace on Mount Olympus. The least known of the Olympians served as the armorer to the pantheon. Hermes' winged helmet and sandals, Achilles' armor, Eros' bow and arrows, and many other magnificent metal works of the Greek stories originated in his forge. Even Ares, the personification of sheer brutality and bloodlust admired his work, admitting the spirit for war was useless without weapons to fight it with.

Hephaestus laid out his supplies on the anvil and stared at them for a while, contemplating which piece of warrior attire to assemble first. He could not recall the last time, if ever, that he had forged anything for a mortal man. Although he received the same lack of attention from the mortals as he did from the gods, he was still determined to do his absolute best on the project, if for no other reason than pride in his craft. His contemplation was soon shattered by the sound of someone trying to leave his palace undetected and he ducked out of sight.

The war god Ares tiptoed his way around the workshop, nervous because he couldn't leave with the same ease he had entered. He noticed everything laid out on the anvil. It wasn't like Hephaestus to leave his forge before finishing a project, but he was relieved that he wouldn't be caught sneaking out after a marathon session of adultery with the smithing god's wife, Aphrodite. This relief was shattered by the next sound he heard.

"Hello Ares. Would you like some food before you go? Or perhaps some wine? You must be hungry and thirsty after all that exertion."

Ares nearly jumped out of his skin at the shock.

"Hephaestus, you're…. what are you doing here?"

"Well Ares, you see, this is my workshop which just happens to be in my palace. It's where I work. And make things, like…. Zeus's lightning bolts, Hermes' sandals, your armor…." Hephaestus said this in the tone of a person explaining that two plus two equals four and not five.

"Yes, I was hoping you'd be here. I need you to forge me a new, um, breast plate. My current one isn't tight enough to show off my muscles."

"Really, you don't need to be evasive with me. I know why you're really here. Don't you remember that time I caught you and my wife in a chain link net and dragged you in front of the rest of the gods to humiliate you?"

"Yes. I mean no. I mean I've never once tapped your wife. We're friends. That's it."

"Ares you're a terrible liar. And everyone knows about the affair. You really don't need to cover it up anymore."

"I'm a little confused here. Shouldn't your response to all this be stay away from my wife or I'll kill you? Not that you could. Or could anyone really. Or I you. After all we're immortal. How are you being so casual about this?"

Hephaestus smiled like that of a man who was enjoying another's discomfort, but not in a malicious way. This had been going on long enough and he decided to clear the air. Now that the Trojan War was over the gods were all very much inclined to go back to whatever they had been up to before. In the case of Hephaestus, he had nothing other than his work and his wife. He loved Aphrodite but his real love was the forge.

"I love my wife, but she is, shall we say, a handful. I don't think any one man can handle her on his own. Having you around takes some of the pressure off. Not that I don't enjoy her as well. The Fates tell me her name

14

will one day be synonymous with things that turn people on. It should also be associated with insatiable appetite, but I'm told the nymphs will be honored with that one."

"I have to agree with you Hephaestus. I've fought many times before but her bedroom is the most punishing battlefield I've ever stepped foot on."

Before Hephaestus could agree or disagree Aphrodite entered the workshop wearing only a toga. Her face had the smile of someone who had indulged her appetite plenty but was still hungry for more. She walked confidently despite her limp. Unlike her husband's deformity this limp was entirely voluntary. The goddess of love looked at both men with surprise and pleasure.

"Ares, you weren't trying to sneak away were you? I'm still able to walk, which means you still have territory to seize, war god." Aphrodite said this as though she had had a delicious lunch only a couple hours before and was already looking forward to a delightful dinner.

Ares couldn't believe what he was hearing, or that she had no problem saying it in front of Hephaestus. This had been their first illicit rendezvous since before the Trojan War. The constant fighting had kept most of the Olympians in a state of voluntary celibacy, as their constant meddling in the affairs of mortals left little time or energy for other endeavors. Aphrodite looked at him like a wolf looks at a rabbit trying to scamper off.

"Like I said, I'm still able to walk and I need that fixed. Ares, either you're coming back upstairs or Hephaestus is going to take me right here. You two work it out but if I don't get an answer soon I'll go find a lucky mortal." With that Aphrodite exited the workshop to return to her bedroom. Ares was astounded.

"Does she realize how little sense that makes? If two GODS can't satisfy her why does think a mortal can?"

"Ares, my wife is the literal embodiment of sexual desire. As long as she has her divine powers she'll always be insatiable."

"So, the only way that'll change is if we're ever replaced as gods?"

"I do believe you understand things correctly. There's a prophecy that it might happen. Hades says Tiresias keeps saying that 'Olympus will fall from a cross'. Of course, we try to make him elaborate but he refuses. Some of us recommend torturing him but that would be rather pointless since he would just go silent. And he's already dead so we can't exactly kill him."

Ares looked over at the wall and saw an outline for some rather unusual looking armor on the wall. It looked familiar yet distinct. His curiosity overwhelmed him. "What's that armor you're working on?" He asked.

"Trojan. Yes, I know they were wiped out. Hades has ordered me to build...."

"New equipment for the survivors? What good would it do them?" Ares said, cutting off Hephaestus before he could finish his sentence. This act annoyed Hephaestus more than Ares fornicating with his wife.

"Oh, it's not for a survivor. It's for one of their fallen. After seeing the mangled body of Astyanax, the son of Prince Hector of Troy, Hades decided to grant a rare furlough to Hector. It will be with the strict provision that Hector may only visit Ithaca, and only then long enough to conduct his necessary business."

Ares had seen many mortal men carry out blood-soaked missions of vengeance. Normally they were against enemy combatants who had recently killed their comrades. In his experience the dead had seen the end of war. He wondered why any one of them would want to continue the cycle even in death. Hephaestus could see the wheels turning in Ares' brain.

"The Ithacan king Odysseus ordered Hector's young son thrown from the walls of Troy to ensure he would not grow up to seek vengeance. When Hades met the boy that was his breaking point. Ares, we're all about to have to answer to the god of the underworld. He's grown rather irritated with the rest of us."

"Even you?"

"Actually no, but that's only because he shows me the same lack of regard as the rest of you. He only speaks to me when he wants something from me. In this case he has requested I forge Hector new warrior attire and weapons for his confrontation with Odysseus. Of course, I will oblige him as I greatly enjoy my work. It's so satisfying to see the exquisite final product after hours of pounding and sweating away in a hot room. I imagine you experienced that same feeling before you tried to sneak out of here."

"Hephaestus, what is the meaning of this? You voice your approval of me conducting carnal business with your wife but then throw jabs sharper than Apollo's arrows, which you also made."

"Settle down Ares. I've merely concluded that it's best to just appreciate the situation for what it is and laugh about it. I already caught and humiliated you both, we're all immortal so killing each other isn't an option."

The wiring in Ares' brain began to short circuit and burn out. He was torn between going back upstairs for another round with Aphrodite and running away to escape the awkwardness of the situation. Hephaestus was manipulating him so much that Ares wondered if he was actually Athena in disguise. Or maybe he was Dionysus-the wine god was the closest thing the Olympians had to the trickster god Loki.

"So we're all going to answer to Hades are we? Are his hands clean?" asked Ares.

"For the most part, yes. I don't believe he's ever even interacted with mortals outside his domain. Other than our meetings at Olympus and that one time he kind of kidnapped his wife, I don't think he's even left the underworld before."

"Kind of kidnapped his wife? He either did or he didn't."

"Reports vary on that one. Even if it was kidnapping that still pales in comparison to what most of us Olympians have done. Hades isn't responsible for any children being murdered."

Ares' face registered the grim realization immediately. He knew that as the god of war he was seen as being responsible for many counts of the same crime. It occurred to him that this might be a good time to reveal what he had seen over the years, but he didn't feel comfortable doing so. While Hephaestus was being surprisingly friendly with him, Ares did not feel the necessary comfort with him to open him up to sharing his deepest secrets.

"Hephaestus, this has been a lot to take in. As much as I would love to get back on top of your wife, I need to leave. I need to consult Athena."

"She's always been a trusted advisor for you, hasn't she? Go on then. Remember, you're welcome here any time Ares. She could easily be your wife." Hephaestus said with a mischievous yet sincere smile.

Ares once again did a double take. It felt like Hephaestus had been trying a similar deception as the Greeks did when they feigned retreat from Troy. The war god then formulated a plan: consult Athena for advice, then consult Dionysus for help to forget. His only question now was in which order should he perform those actions.

CHAPTER FOUR

JUSTICE AND VENGEANCE

"Sooner or later everyone sits down to a banquet of consequences."
-Robert Louis Stevenson, Scottish author

I thaca. Thirteen years after the end of the Trojan War. The great King Odysseus sat on his reclaimed throne next to his wife Penelope. His success at slaying the men who tried to take his wife and kingdom while he was presumed dead had deterred all challengers in the previous three years. Ithaca had become a prosperous kingdom under his leadership. No one dared messed with *the* Odysseus, slayer of nobles and destroyer of Troy.

This success came with its own problems, however. While the Ithacan kings' demeanor and bearing still projected wisdom and authority, his appearance did not. He had the look of a once formidable man who no longer maintained himself. He still wore a sword most of the time, but it was now more of an affectation and status symbol than a practical tool. His mind had always been his greatest asset anyway, and like most kings, surrounded himself with armed men who looked like death incarnate.

As Odysseus held court, one of his sons, Telemachus, approached him with a worried expression. Odysseus anticipated the young man would inform him of a matter of grave importance to the kingdom that he could easily solve, but he would pretend as though it were a challenge.

"Father, there's a peasant outside requesting to see you. He has traveled a great distance he says. He has been wronged so severely that only *you* can set this matter right."

"Very well, escort him in here."

His palace guards ushered in a man of average height and lean build, or at least that's what could be inferred. His heavy robes obscured most of his outward appearance, and he moved in a way that suggested he was capable of rapid speed but chose to be slow and deliberate. The man approached Odysseus and stopped close enough to read every expression on his face, but not close enough to make him uncomfortable. Still, everyone present knew most did not step this close to the king. But somehow, no one showed any inclination to challenge him.

"Great and wise King Odysseus, I have come from far away to see you. I am but a humble farmer. My land was seized by bandits. They stabbed me and threw me into the sea. By the grace of Poseidon, I survived. When I finally made my way home, it was destroyed. My farm was salvageable, but my family was not. My neighbor witnessed all of it. He said the raiders killed my son to ensure he would not pursue them in the future."

"Someone dared do this in MY KINGDOM? I shall send troops wherever necessary to right this injustice! I'll have those men slaughtered without mercy!"

"Funny you should say that Your Majesty. By that logic, your guards should run you through with spears and swords and mount your head on a pike."

"How dare you speak to me in such a manner! Who are you to....."

The peasant answered by lowering his hood and showing his face to all present. None of them save Odysseus had ever personally met Hermes, messenger of the gods, in person before, but instinctively, they knew. His eyes gave off a vibe of authority that couldn't come from any mortal man or even demigod. The Ithacans braced themselves for his next words, fearful of the message he come to deliver.

"Great Odysseus. Feared and admired ruler of Ithaca. Slayer of nobles, destroyer of Troy. Beloved husband and father. Favored child of Athena. I'm sure by now all your people have heard how you conceived the Trojan Horse, incurred Poseidon's wrath on your way home, and were waylaid by sea monsters, sirens, sorceresses, and many other obstacles. It's not immodest to boast of such deeds, is it Odysseus?"

"Which of the gods sent you, Hermes? Poseidon already enacted his vengeance for blinding his bastard cyclops. Has he decided that my perilous journey was not sufficient punishment?"

"I was sent not by Poseidon but Hades."

"The ruler of the Underworld? Why? I had his permission to enter and consult Tiresias. Has *he* now decided I committed an affront to him?"

"The god of the Underworld does not normally punish men while they walk among the living, but in your case, he has decided to make an exception. You did everything you did after the war to make your way home to your wife and son. Ironically, I am here because of another son you reunited with *his* father."

Hermes extended his right hand in front of him and projected an image for all to see. A Greek soldier hoisted a young boy and threw him. The child was shown in slow motion in a free fall. At the end of the fall, he no longer looked human. Sand, blood, and dirt intermingled freely all over him. His head was mostly intact, and his eye gave off a look as though the light had been extinguished, as indeed it had been.

"I'm sure you still remember Astyanax, don't you Odysseus? You convinced your fellow Greeks that he was too dangerous to be left alive. You believed he would seek revenge. Yet, you are currently surrounded by men who seem they could have been sired by Ares himself. How exactly was he a threat?"

Odysseus' mouth opened wider than the gates of Troy after the horse had infiltrated. His wife and son looked at him the way a Trojan refugee might. They knew he had killed in battle, of course, and that non-combatants had died. While neither were completely ignorant of the harsh reality of war, they wondered how the wise man they loved could have arrived at the decision that it was necessary to eliminate a helpless child. Hermes did not wait for him to answer.

"Do not bother with explaining yourself to me, Odysseus. I am merely a messenger of the gods. Hades is quite eager to meet you. You will have to justify your actions to him. Be warned: ever since the fall of Troy, he has been far less neutral. Even Athena, with all her wisdom, likely won't be able to think up an explanation that will work for you there."

Odysseus desperately hoped this man was an impostor.

"Seize him!" he ordered.

The guards didn't move a step towards Hermes before he threw up his left hand and forced their blades to each other's throats. Hermes casually held his hand up with apparently minimal effort whiles his eyes glowed with the fire normally shown by Ares. Odysseus now lost all hope that this was a hoax.

"It would be most unfortunate to paint the walls of your throne room with the blood of these men, Odysseus. You will receive another visitor at this time tomorrow. Sharpen your sword and string your bow. You'll need them. If anyone blocks this visitor from coming to you, Apollo will unleash the same plague he hit the Greek army with years ago on the shores of Troy. And while you explain your actions to your family, don't forget to mention what you did immediately after you left Troy."

With his message fully delivered, small wings protruded from Hermes' sandals and the messenger of the gods flew away. Everyone present was relieved to see him go as it meant he was done delivering bad news. Penelope and Telemachus left the room to process the new knowledge they had been confronted with. Odysseus was left with only the knowledge that his end was near.

CHAPTER FIVE

BOOMERANG

"The axe forgets, but the tree remembers."
-African proverb

The journey felt like an eternity. Then maybe it felt like mere moments. Hector couldn't be sure. His perception of time had dulled ever since his death. Without the rising and setting of the sun, the departure and return of spring and harvest, watching people be born or grow old and die, or the human sleep cycle for reference, the passage of time now felt foreign to him.

As the sun warmed his skin and the wind and waves of the Mediterranean Sea blew in his hair and rocked the boat, he began to regain memories of feeling the sensations experienced by mortal living men. One element of his mortal life, however, felt like the warm embrace of an old friend. Hades had ordered Hephaestus to supply Hector with a fresh new set of warrior garb.

Hector's new accoutrements were the ideal for a fighting man on foot. Shoulder and breast plates that provided adequate protection while feeling as light as a feather, especially when worn by a well-conditioned soldier. A helmet with the gleaming crest of Troy and metal that cooled the wearer's head. A shield made of the finest bronze, emblazoned with a horse rearing back on both legs, representing the vanquished nation of Troy riding into battle one last time. Its perimeter featured engravings of everyone near and dear to him who perished in the Trojan War.

Everything he wore was custom made for him, to fit him so well it was though it had formed around him as he grew into a man. The short sword on his hip felt like a trusted ally had rejoined him. His spear looked like it could level buildings if thrown hard enough. Both had been tested by Cerberus. Hephaestus liked to use the guard beast to test the strength of his products. If Hades' pet couldn't destroy them, then neither could any mortal.

The boatman, Charon, found the territory more unfamiliar than Hector did. The ongoing task of transporting the recently deceased to the Underworld usually kept him from venturing far into the land of men. He couldn't even recall the last time he set eyes on a living human being. Today however, his task had been reversed on Hades' order. Delivering a dead man to the world of the living felt like madness.

Soon, the boat landed at port in Ithaca. Though Troy was thirteen years gone, the stories of the ferocity of its soldiers still circulated throughout the Greek world. This was to be expected as returning warriors are keen to exalt their enemies as a way of exalting themselves. The Ithacans present scattered at the sight of Hector in his battle dress. While one soldier was hardly an invading army, one from Troy was cause for alarm. After all, their king and his army had supposedly taken no prisoners, so a Trojan warrior could only have come from the place they desperately hoped to avoid.

Hector and Charon marched onward to the palace. Charon was quite perplexed at the sight of living people running away from him. No one had ever been *happy* to see him, but they came to him without complaint as all the dead knew getting in his boat was inevitable. As the two walked, the temperature in the air dropped and clouds began to obscure the sun. Their mere presence disrupted the natural order of things.

One man even froze at the sight of Hector. He had never seen his face, but he remembered well what Trojan armor looked like. There was something familiar about his eyes. It dawned on him that he had been on guard duty the day Achilles defeated Hector in single combat. He had seen Hector dragged back to the Greek camp behind a chariot, broken bloodied, and dead. How could he then be walking through Ithaca in gleaming armor with no signs of injury or even ageing?

The Greek veteran never found out whether his old enemy remembered him. He was able to proceed to the palace without running but with the speed nearly that of a horse, as his armor felt nearly weightless. Upon his arrival at the gate, the palace guards allowed the two of them entry, unchallenged. Palace staff dispersed just like the people who saw them at the docks as they instinctively knew he was the visitor Hermes warned them about.

Odysseus stood inside his throne room in his old battle gear. It fit him snugly, reminding him of the weight he had gained since he returned from the war. The favor of the gods and lack of surviving enemies (in Greece or elsewhere) had made it unnecessary to pick up a sword or bow except for the occasional hunt with his son. For the last three years, he had needed little of the cunning or tenacity that made him the decorated warrior and strategist he was.

Hector arrived inside and surveyed his old foe with a mixture of pity, anger, resentment, bloodlust, and mutual respect. Every emotion he had ever felt when he was alive flooded him at once. The Underworld had dulled these feelings, but the sight of the man who prematurely reunited him with his son, sitting at the throne of a prosperous kingdom, enraged him more than anything he experienced in life. All that limited Hector's rage was seeing Odysseus as a fellow royal and warrior.

"Do you know who I am, Odysseus?"

"Yes. Hector, right? How are you here? I last saw you in the Underworld!"

"Hades. He's not the mad deity you believe him to be, no. He granted me special passage here. He decided it wasn't right that you get to live out the rest of your life here, free of hardship and pain, while your family and subjects see you as almost a god. Hades was merciful in that he decided to give you what you denied my son: an opportunity to defend yourself. Let's see if you can defeat one last Trojan!"

Hector hurled his spear as he had so many times on previous battlefields. Odysseus raised his shield to deflect it, rendering the shield useless. The throwing weapon shattered it after pushing it backward into Odysseus's face. Odysseus discarded the broken shield and ran towards Hector with maximum effort but less than maximum results. Sitting on the throne all those years had weakened his legs. The lack of practice weakened his proficiency with the sword.

Odysseus fought valiantly but futilely. Within minutes, he was nearing the end of his aerobic capacity. Hector pushed him around the room, delaying the inevitable end to the duel. He had waited thirteen years; he could wait a bit longer. Odysseus looked as though he had done the equivalent exertion to climbing the walls of Troy, while Hector appeared to have expended no energy at all.

Eventually, Odysseus managed to land the first strike. His blade managed to pierce Hector's shoulder but not a drop of blood came out. Suddenly, Hector figured out the real reason everything felt so awkward since leaving the Underworld: he wasn't actually alive again. His armor had been redundant all along as he was still dead, and with no blood flowing through his veins, no weapon could harm him.

The former prince of Troy saw that his enemy was nearing death by exhaustion. He could not allow the battle to end that way. Hector grabbed Odysseus' sword with his bare hand and discarded it. The next strike would have been worthy of an epic poem on its own had any mortal men witnessed it. Hector stabbed Odysseus through his heart. Odysseus' breast plate was scarcely an obstacle; Hector's sword sliced through it like silk on both ends.

Ithaca's favorite warrior king would have been brought to his knees had the sword not nailed him to the wall. Hector had the advantages of a seasoned warrior's proficiency with the weapon, the rage of a father who had lost a son, and the absence of human vulnerabilities. These factors combined to form a fighter as invulnerable as Ares. Had Hades not limited Hector's permitted time back on Earth, Hector could have single handedly crushed all the Greek city states. He surveyed his defeated enemy with a mixture of satisfaction, pity, and finality.

"This didn't have to happen, Odysseus. I didn't have any ill will for what you did to Troy. Ultimately, you and all your countrymen will later join me in the Underworld anyway. This was for my son. He would have been raised in slavery, with the short life span common to even royalty of our day; you weren't likely to live long enough for him to be a later threat anyway. Even if you did, you have guards who would have been my equal in battle when I was alive."

Odysseus looked at Hector with resignation. His eyes knew his life was ending while his body continued to fight. The bleeding, convulsing, and shaking were the body's involuntary response to trauma evoked when the mind knows it's over, but the body won't accept it. The blade had pierced his bottom two ribs and sliced the bottom tenth of his heart, the only reason death hadn't occurred instantaneously.

"I thought of throwing you from the walls like you did to Astyanax, but that would have been too impersonal. Ares and Athena interceded on your behalf with Hades. They felt you still a warrior and deserved the dignity of falling in battle. It didn't surprise me that Athena still favored you after what you did. She disfigured and banished a rape victim to a distant island once, so it figures a murderer would be her kind of man."

Blood began to spew from Odysseus' mouth. His hands were now dyed red from trying to extract the blade from his upper abdominal/lower chest area. If not for the sword holding him to the wall, he would have slipped in the puddle of his own urine that now stained the floor. Hector decided this was enough and removed his helmet to make sure his face was the last thing he would see and knocked him unconscious. Charon stepped forward after silently observing the fatal showdown.

"We must leave now Hector. Hades was quite clear about the terms of your parole. Only long enough to avenge the boy. You saw how the weather abruptly changed here when we arrived."

"I haven't quite finished with him, Charon."

During the brief exchange between the two, Odysseus' body had finally expired. Hector found an axe on the wall behind the throne, raised the blade far above his head and swung it into Odysseus' neck like a baseball bat. The spine proved as weak as tissue paper and the head flew all the way across the room. Hector picked up the severed head and looked to his divinely conscripted attendant.

"Pick up the body, Charon."

Hector and Charon walked out of the throne room. Hector placed his helmet back on and carried Odysseus' head like a quarterback would a football. Charon carried the body like a sack of flour over his shoulder. He trailed behind Hector as they made their way out of the palace and towards the palace entrance. The guards who saw them raised their spears, knowing they would be no match for the undead soldier, but wanting to depart the earth like warriors.

"I have killed your king. I believe that makes *me* the king for the short time I'll be here. If that doesn't convince you...."

Hector placed the head on the ground and removed his armor. He then drew his sword and ran it through his abdomen. The guards had not seen a weapon used in battle in many years. After all, it had been a peaceful place since their king had returned, but they were more taken aback by Hector remaining upright. He showed no signs of pain and spilled no blood.

"Hades allowed me to come here from the Underworld to seek justice for my son. Your beloved king murdered him after the war ended. Your weapons are useless against me. Hades also believes that mortal men shouldn't have to suffer and die for the actions of rulers most of them will never meet. Our nations aren't at war so trying to kill me would be pointless for you. Leave a spear and I won't take you to the Underworld with me."

The Ithacan soldiers accepted his terms unconditionally. They decided Charon could wait a few years to meet them. Hector placed the king's remains in the middle of the entranceway and drove a spear shaft through the side of the ribs that his sword hadn't punctured, forming a base of support to turn it into a pole. Then he affixed Odysseus' head to the other end.

The palace staff came out from hiding and recoiled in horror at the sight of their fallen king. Each of them looked at Hector with the same fear they would look at a monster like the Hydra, the Minotaur, or the Chimaera. Some of them even dropped to one knee, hoping that submitting would spare them the wrath of this unstoppable enemy.

"Do not fear me, people of Ithaca. I am not *your* enemy. I know none of *you* were responsible for the slaughter of my family and my countrymen. None of you benefitted from the looting of the palace I spent most of my life in. Lord Hades will not allow me to stay here and assume the throne— not that I want to anyway. The throne I intended to pursue is now a pile of ash across the sea. Spread the message across the Greek world. The criteria for banishment to Tartarus has been expanded. Rulers who play with human lives like a child plays with toys *will* be punished for it. The Trojan War is now truly over."

CHAPTER SIX

THE TRIAL OF ODYSSEUS

"For the powerful, crimes are those that others commit."
-Noam Chomsky, American linguist,
philosopher and activist

O dysseus stepped off Charon's small boat into the entrance of the Underworld. The guard dog Cerberus' heads stared at him with fear, confusion, and familiarity. He rarely saw the same human being cross his path twice. If the dog could think as a man, he would have wondered, "Why does this man already look as though I thrashed him thoroughly? The last time he was here, my master instructed me to allow him to leave unharmed. Wait—he's covered in blood, yet his arms and legs remain attached to him. *I* would have ripped off his limbs. It must have been an especially ferocious man that did it."

The now dead Ithacan king was now equal to the lowest peasant. His cunning and genius could only delay his arrival here so much. The Trojan army, the cyclops and Circe, the wrath of Poseidon, Scylla and Charybdis, Calypso and Helios, most of which still menaced all manner of men in the mortal world, couldn't combine to keep him away from his beloved homeland forever. It was a bitter irony that the one enemy of his he thought vanquished for good would be the one to permanently tear him away from his beloved wife and son.

While making his way down a damp, darkened corridor he was greeted by the sight of a bronze bull statue the size of the horse that infiltrated Troy. The statue made bellowing noises like its flesh and blood counterpart. Two cloaked figures suddenly appeared under its stomach and opened a door underneath to pull out a human male. Odysseus couldn't believe his eyes when he saw Telemachus, the statue must have converted his screaming into bull sounds!

This shouldn't have been possible; after all, his son was still among the living. Nevertheless, Telemachus looked as though he had been burning in fire heated just enough to take an exceptionally long time to cook him to death. Somehow, he did not look to his father to save him. Odysseus reasoned that it might be a hallucination brought about by the blow to the head from Hector's helmet. Fortunately (depending on your perspective), he didn't have to wonder long as Hades had appeared to greet him.

"Great Odysseus of Ithaca, come to join me down here at last! I'm going to spare you one torment, for now at least. What you just saw wasn't real and it wasn't a vision brought about by your damaged brain. No part of you is damaged anymore, for you are dead. It was a projection created by me. Don't worry. Unlike mortal men, I never allow sons to be punished for the crimes of their fathers."

"Crimes? I have committed no crimes. All my actions were just."

"Were they? There are some people here who would strongly disagree!"

With that, Hades escorted Odysseus to his throne room and took a seat. Odysseus was then confronted by a horde of bloody people. They looked somewhat familiar, obviously not Greek but not obviously anything else. The smaller group of men accompanying them were more than obviously Greek, they wore the armor of Ithacan soldiers.

"Do you even remember who any of these people were? I'll give you a hint: you were responsible for all their deaths. Ah, I see your confusion. I'm going to have to be more specific, aren't I? Do you remember the Cicones, Odysseus?"

"I can't say that I do."

"Are you sure? You were quite keen on punishing them for their alliance with Troy!"

"Ah, yes, I do recall now. They sided with Troy during the war. They had to pay," Odysseus said this with the same tone a man might recount his most recent meal.

"You escaped punishment for this action in life, depending on one's perspective. Ares was kind enough to provide me with a "battlefield" report. You lost six men per ship in that action. The small number you see here were just the ones that got buried. The souls of the rest are still swimming through the Mediterranean after their bodies were tossed away like refuse. I still send Charon out there from time to time to recover them. Poseidon will not help."

"As I said, they had to pay for siding with Troy."

"But why? The war was over! You had won; Troy was in ruins! What could you possibly have gained from continuing the conflict with this much smaller group!?"

"The usual things: pillaging, elimination of threats, keeping my men sharp," Odysseus answered.

"One day, Odysseus, men like you won't be able to do the things you've done without repercussions. It's a shame that men like you often escape consequences until you meet me. The Fates have shown me some rather unique visions of humanity's future."

Hades held up his left hand as Hermes had done in the Ithacan palace and projected a series of images of men in grey and black uniforms with small skulls on them, all repeating in a strange language that was translated for Odysseus' ears, "I was only following orders."

"You were the higher authority giving those orders, Odysseus. A soldier in battle must obey orders and often faces the same treatment as his enemy if he refuses, no matter how wrong they are. Your men had no choice but to follow you into battle if they wanted to return home. Therefore, I shall not punish them for your command decisions."

Hades then abruptly waved his right hand and a large gap opened beneath the feet of the dead Ithacan soldiers. The shocked warriors fell and let out a blood curling scream as their bodies dropped into a lake of fire. Hades looked gratified as though he had just watched a murderer sentenced to death for a decade's old murder, indeed more so as he was the sentencing judge in this case.

"I've been waiting for a long time to do that, Odysseus. I wanted to do it immediately upon their arrival, but I thought you should witness it personally. Before the Trojan War, all the dead spent their eternity here, equally, except for the very best and very worst. I've decided to expand the criteria for banishment to torture in Tartarus and the paradise that is the Elysian Fields."

Odysseus remained his stoic self despite his inner fear.

"I'm confused. You said you weren't going to punish those men for my command decisions. If you were being truthful, then why did you send them to Tartarus?"

"As punishment for their conduct which was not necessary for war! They didn't just kill armed men; that I could forgive even if Ares wouldn't insist on it. No, it was that they used the unwilling widows of the men they had killed to satisfy their carnal urges! They tried to bring *human beings* home with them as trophies. It wasn't enough for these soldiers to rape them once; they wanted to bring them to their homes so they could do it at their leisure for the rest of their lives!"

"That is the way of war, Hades. The victors take what they want. That is how it will always be," Odysseus said with the certainty of man predicting the sun would rise the next day.

"No, Odysseus, it will not. Oh yes, it will continue to happen through history but there will come a day when the most powerful military force will not tolerate it."

Hades once again projected an image from his hand. In this projection, two young men in brown looking soldiers' uniforms with red, white, and blue cloth on their shoulders were shown discovering a room full of green paper. Odysseus had no idea what this paper was, but the soldiers had the same facial expression Agamemnon did when he finally discovered the Trojan treasure room.

"Why are they so elated at the discovery of parchment?"

"In the future, most human societies will use paper currency to replace the gold and silver coins they have now. These soldiers will come across a large amount of this paper currency. The Fates believe it will have been the property of a vicious foreign tyrant who stole most of it from his own people. There is more to see, Odysseus."

The scene in the vision shifted. Now the young soldiers found themselves facing down an older one. The older soldier had the same facial expression Achilles had when he learned his cousin Patroclus had been slain by the Greeks. Odysseus had no idea what any of the markings on their uniforms meant. The name "Blount" did not sound like a great warrior. He inferred by the presence of armed guards behind him and the two stars on his armor that the old soldier intended to hand down punishment to the younger ones.

"One day, Odysseus, humanity will learn to move beyond what you did. I could maybe forgive your actions on Cikone as the byproduct of a protracted armed conflict, as at least there you fought against armed men. However, you will still burn for eternity for your last act in Troy. Persephone, bring in the boy!"

Hades' loyal wife entered the throne room hand-in-hand with a small, bloody and mangled child. Persephone stared at Odysseus with a look of contempt she had previously reserved only for her domineering mother. In her role as wife of the ruler of the Underworld, she took it upon herself to accompany Charon whenever he had to transport children. The boatman was a rather scary looking figure and Persephone's gentle and beautiful appearance helped to persuade them into the boat.

"Explain yourself, Odysseus. Did you think this child a smaller version of Achilles? Did the Trojans infect him with a dangerous plague to spread wherever he landed in Greece? HE WAS NO SOLDIER AND THE WAR WAS ALREADY OVER!"

"You are correct. He was no soldier—at that time. He was too dangerous to be left alive. I simply informed the other Greek kings that years later they might one morning wake up with their throats cut by him as revenge. He would likely have tried to avenge his father later."

"Ah, yes, perhaps you are right on that. After all, your son did avenge you. Correction, he merely searched for you. He did not scour the world looking to massacre anyone that might be a threat to you. No, he merely killed *adult men* who sought to kill him and marry his mother, whether she liked it or not!"

"Once again, you confuse me Hades. How exactly does that make *my* actions worse? What is your point here?"

"Either way, Odysseus, you did not think things through. Astyanax would have been a mere eleven years old when you arrived home at Troy. He would have been kept as a slave child in the land of the man who brought his mother home as a war prize. He would likely not even have learned to wield a sword! Even if he somehow did so in secret, how would he have made the journey to Ithaca? And even for royalty, life spans are quite short for most mortals. What made you think you'd still be alive when the boy was old enough to seek revenge?"

"You have no idea what I had endured up to that point, god of the Underworld. Do you even experience the passage of time? How could you? You're eternal and ageless. For ten. Complete. Years. I camped on the beaches of Troy. I watched my friends and countrymen fight, bleed, and die. You and your family *can't* bleed or die. My main priority was to keep myself and my soldiers *alive*. I had to balance this *every day* with the mission at hand. Passing between Scylla and Charybdis hardly phased me because I had encountered so many situations where no matter what decision I made men under me would die and all I could hope for was to make one that resulted in fewer losses. Even as a commander directing troops, I was not insulated from the sight of their bodies being hacked, slashed, and mangled. The truces arranged for both sides to bury their dead never came soon enough to stop the smell of rotting remains baking in the Trojan heat to fall over all of us like a massive rain. Eventually, we were desensitized to it all. The child you've brought in to shame me merely looks like a smaller version of what I saw nearly every day for ten years. I literally saw much of the sand run red with blood—Trojan and Greek, exalted officers and ordinary soldiers; it all mingled together just the same."

Hades stopped and meditated on Odysseus' words. He waved his right hand and a portal opened to a lush green fertile valley full of happy looking people. Persephone ushered Astyanax through and off the boy went. She then took a seat next to Hades' throne and observed, curious about the man who orchestrated the great Trojan migration to the Underworld.

"Odysseus, you have given much to consider. Either way, the boy doesn't deserve this dark place. He will spend eternity unaware of everything that led to his arrival here. Either way, I cannot allow him to spend forever among those who killed him. I am considering amending your fate here. Now go and join..."

"I was not finished, Hades. No, you and your kind have no idea what it was like, but I am not through enlightening you. Do you know what was worse than the sights and sounds and smell of battle? Most of the men killed, screamed for their mothers or wives but those that survived did it far more—silently. For a while, all most of us could think about between battles was getting back home to our families. We did what all soldiers do to cope. When we could get wine, we drank it. We cooked our food, cleaned our camps, played games, maintained our equipment. The higher ups like myself attended numerous strategy meetings. We did everything we could to keep the longing away. Some of the men thought about their families less as the war went on. Others thought of them more. For some, even the images of their loved ones began to fade from their minds. Many believed they would only reunite with them *here*. Regardless of how they coped, all of them experienced hardships most humans and none of the gods ever have. The muscle tissue of their bodies devouring itself as it's been deprived of nutrition for long stretches. Dehydration so bad they would crawl to the nearest corpse and imbibe the blood. They could not tell the blood from water. The wounded who survived and continued to fight could no longer do simple things like rise from their beds in the morning without being reminded that part of them was pierced by a sword, an arrow, or a spear. Before I conceived the horse from watching a soldier carve a small one for his son, the Trojans seemed protected like your brethren on Mount Olympus. And even those few Greeks who remained, who received the gift of one day casting off their armor and shields and returning to peaceful life at home with their families, bore the curse of memory. Even the least intelligent man who survives battle has total recall of it. Most will never again sleep through the night without reliving the horrors unless they drown them out with wine. There are certain sights sounds and smells you never forget. On their best days, they manage to gain enough distance that the memory of the war feels more like a story described to them second hand. Are you beginning to understand, Hades?"

"As you have been candid with me, Odysseus, I shall do the same with you. There is good reason the Trojans seemed as protected as the gods on Olympus. Was it not believed that the Trojan walls could not have been built by men?"

Odysseus had an idea of the explanation to follow. The impregnable nature of Troy's walls had fertilized the growth of the Trojan horse in his mind. The idea had sprung from his mind the way Athena had from Zeus' head. Like most mortals, he believed it would never be known for sure how they were so tall and strong. Now, he would learn the answer to the mystery.

"Long ago, the Olympians were as divided as the city states of Greece.

Hera united us under the realization that we never officially sanctioned Zeus' supremacy. We chained him up and took over but his old allies from our war with the Titans freed him. As punishment for their treason, he sentenced Poseidon and Apollo to hard labor. By the time they had been punished to his satisfaction, the walls of Troy came to be. I apologize for how we inadvertently prolonged the war, Odysseus."

"So, one of the gods who built Troy helped its defenders while the other aided the attackers. Did it occur to either of them that they were cancelling each other out?"

"War has a way of inflaming passions and impairing reason and logic, Odysseus. Even us gods are vulnerable from time to time."

"Yet unlike *you*, Hades, most of them don't get enraged until it personally offends them. Your brother was quite the patron of the Greeks until I blinded that cyclops love child of his. Never mind that the giant bastard intended to eat me."

"As I recall, you and your men had trespassed in his home and tried to steal his food."

"We were merely trying to survive. You wouldn't know about that. Neither would he."

"I never considered these things, Odysseus. For the sake of fairness, I ask you to consider what I have seen. Did any of the combatants in the Trojan War even *notice* my apparent lack of involvement? It would have been pointless for *me* to intervene. Everyone involved would eventually come to me regardless of the outcome. Unlike my relatives, I have seen every single result. I don't mean the fall of nations—I mean the broken and battered men you saw dying on the battlefield."

Odysseus looked on in agreement and shock, taken by surprise that he had common ground with the god of the dead.

"The children broke me, Odysseus. My domain is a place they are not intended to enter. You mortals have not figured out how to keep your children alive until adulthood. For a while, they were sent here by disease. Sometimes, they were boys who believed themselves to be men and took up arms. Then the Trojan War..."

"What about it?"

"Troy got desperate enough that it began conscripting children. Boys as young as 12 plucked from their homes and handed ill fitting armor and

35

weapons too large for them. The Trojans tried to keep them in reserve, but you Greeks often wrecked those plans. The Fates often show us gods visions specific to us. I have seen visions of funeral practices across time. Ares has seen visions of war. He tells me that many nations will resort to this practice in the coming centuries. I could still *almost* accept the child soldiers being sent to me. Then the sack of Troy...."

Odysseus looked at him, wondering what could possibly have broken Hades that night.

"I have received influxes of dead many times over, Odysseus. Mostly uniformed, fighting men. In most wars, the women and children usually manage to flee before soldiers find them. After the Greeks left behind the rubble of Troy, well.... Persephone, tell him."

Persephone looked as though she were now being forced to relive a nightmare. Her face went from terror at the memory to resignation at its normalcy in rapid succession.

"Since I came to the Underworld, I have assisted the ferryman Charon with his duties. Children usually find him terrifying, so I go ashore and shepherd them into the boat. Those are just the ones that have been properly buried and thus make it to the River Styx. When Troy fell, so many of the Trojans had no idea if their children accompanied them here or not. Charon and I recovered a great deal of remains after the Greeks set sail for home. Have you ever seen a baby so severely burned that you couldn't tell it apart from rubble? Your countrymen hacked and mangled children as efficiently they did warriors."

"As I told your husband, we had been fighting for ten long years before that. I won't bother repeating myself beyond that."

Hades looked as though the gravity of the conversations he'd had with Odysseus were beginning to weigh on him heavily. This seemed like the right moment to end the proceedings, for now.

"You have given me much to think about, Odysseus. Perhaps I will not condemn you to eternal punishment as I planned. However, there remain many others who must answer for their actions. I may call on you for counsel in the days to come. In the meantime, I think the usual afterlife is sufficient for you."

CHAPTER SEVEN

WHO'S NEXT?

"The greatest wealth a man can have is an understanding wife."
-*Euripedes*, Author of The Trojan Women

Hades sat on his throne awhile and pondered some more. Odysseus was merely the first confrontation he intended to have. Persephone noticed his quiet contemplation. The weight he was carrying was enough to crush even a god. Usually she had no perception of time while in the Underworld, but the sight of her husband's frozen contemplation was too much to handle.

"How shall we proceed, my lord?"

"If I knew that, I would have already proceeded. I had planned to simply confront Odysseus with his crimes and then banish him to Tartarus, but he hit me with a force as strong as my brother's lightning bolts. Perhaps us gods should not judge mortal men too harshly, if at all. He was right, we the immortal have never felt hunger, fear, privation, or any of the other afflictions of man. As we are immune to these things, why should we be allowed to pass judgement?"

"Yes, Hades, but remember: men live their lives with the daily intent of not offending you. Perhaps the problem with the gods is that they seem to care not what humans do to each other until it personally offends them. After all, didn't your niece revoke her support for the Greeks at the end of the war?"

"That is correct, Persephone. Athena cared not about the many acts of sexual assault that were committed during the sack of Troy until one of them was in *her* temple. If Ajax the Lesser had raped Cassandra just outside the holy site, she wouldn't even know his name. I don't know which is worse, that or her handling of Medusa. Poseidon should be the one in total isolation from everyone for many years, not her."

"Oh, yes, Cassandra. Our dear nephew deserves another millennium of hard labor after his interaction with her. Now, I've heard two versions of this story. In one, he gave Cassandra the gift of prophecy and then she refused his advances. In the other, he merely made a pass at her with no proposition and she declined. Either way, the curse where she would always be right but never believed doomed Troy," Persephone answered.

"Apollo must have seen it as a fair consequence for breaking the deal," Hades argued. "On the surface, it was, but he should have walked back his own actions. As soon as Cassandra said if the boy lives, Troy will burn, he should have shown some compassion. His vindictiveness condemned an entire nation to die."

"But had she been believed, the Trojans would have done the same thing to survive that the Greeks did to ensure they never rose again," Persephone pointed out.

"What do you mean, Persephone?"

"They would have thrown Paris from the walls."

"Thus, the troubling question of whether it is acceptable to trade lives. I fear the gods of Olympus have placed humanity in a Scylla and Charybdis at all times. Any decision they make will somehow result in a terrible outcome."

"The problem is that no one involved thought far ahead. Mortals and gods alike thought not about the ripple effect but their own personal glory. Hades, I think I know where to start. Hera, Athena, and Aphrodite. Wasn't their feud the first of the pebbles that started this avalanche?" Persephone suggested.

"Yes, it was. And Artemis escalated things. We must bring them here to answer for it. I could confront them on Mount Olympus, but if all of us are present, the chaos could level the mortal world. I cannot punish gods as Zeus can, but perhaps I can make them feel the full impact of what they've done."

CHAPTER EIGHT

ARTEMIS ANSWERS
FOR HER ACTIONS

"We are all victims of war, and we all count."
-Marla Ruzicka, activist, aide worker and founder,
Campaign for Innocent Victims in Conflict

Artemis arrived in Hades' throne room short of breath and patience. She couldn't believe what had happened. Having three heads should have made Cerberus an easier target to hit. With her quiver empty and sword drawn, she moved around like one of the warriors hunting Medusa. The chase had irritated her enough that she intended to stab the next thing she saw, whether it was her quarry or not. The next thing she saw was the ceiling get higher as she was knocked to the floor.

The goddess of the hunt found herself pinned to the ground and desperately trying to push the three heads away from her. Each head growled but did not seem interested in devouring her as she would expect. This didn't stop her from gripping the left and right heads with her powerful hands and throwing the best head butt she could at the middle one. Then the struggle suddenly ended.

"Cerberus, heel!"

With that command, the fearsome guard-beast's demeanor became that of an eager puppy, happy to see his master. For Cerberus, all was right with his world whenever Hades or Persephone came into a room. Hades had to stay away from him when he was guarding the entrance to the Underworld. After all, Cerberus wasn't an effective guard when he was excited. The loyal hound rolled over, hoping to get his belly scratched.

Artemis got to her feet and secured her sword. She knew Hades would never be so lax in his duties as to let the dog run free anywhere, so Cerberus had to have been acting on his orders. The beast had approached her and the nymphs in the spring, much the way Actaeon had, only intentionally. She could not turn Cerberus into a stag the way she had the mortal man, so she resorted to her usual problem-solving method.

All her arrows missed, so she called Apollo for help. The sun god tried his best to slay the beast, although he should have realized his arrows would be no more effective against Hades' beloved pet. The two chased him on foot all the way to the River Styx. Apollo would have happily accompanied his sister on the raid but did not want to answer to Zeus the next morning for failing to drag the sun across the sky.

Artemis became overtaken with a mixture of curiosity, annoyance, and fear. Hades was usually absent when the gods convened on Mount Olympus and they rarely (if ever) visited him. When they did, it was usually in response to an overt invitation. As his power was rivaled only by Poseidon and Zeus, they dared not refuse his requests. Why had he used the beast to get her here?

"Hello, Artemis. You haven't been here in a while, have you?"

"I am the goddess of the hunt, the wilderness, of wild animals, the Moon, and of chastity. All those things concern the *living* world, Hades, *not* the *under* world. Why have you brought me here?"

"To answer for what you have done. I don't even know where to begin with you, Artemis. I don't believe any of us have failed in our duty as much as you have."

"*I* have failed? If anyone else spoke to me that way, I would feed him to his own dogs!"

"Like you did with Actaeon? You turned him into a stag and his dogs devoured him after… Now, I've heard different reports here. One of them said he tried to force himself on you, another said he merely stumbled onto the sight of you bathing. Tell me, which is true?"

"I don't know—I've had many men ripped apart. I don't usually learn their names."

"If he tried to force himself on you, then I understand. Otherwise, you escalated it beyond where it needed to go. Men will one day have the wisdom to draw up boundary lines to warn each other where it is not acceptable to go. Why couldn't you do the same?"

"I'm not a mortal. I have no such obligations."

"Of course, you don't. Yet, as a child, you asked your father to grant you ten wishes. What was the tenth?" Hades asked this question as a lawyer would—don't ask any question you don't already know the answer to.

"To have the ability to help women in the pains of childbirth."

"Should it not then be expected that you would not inflict *other* sorts of pain on women?"

"I never have."

"Clytemnestra would disagree."

"Who was she?"

"Iphigenia's mother," Hades' voice went from stern, yet calm, to a tone with which a man might draw a sword and vow not to return it to its sheath until it was coated with the blood of his enemy. Artemis' face said she still had no idea.

"The wife of Agamemnon!" Hades said this with the rage of a man who had just learned that not only had his wife committed adultery against him but did so with his brother.

"In peacetime, sons bury their fathers, Artemis. In war, fathers bury their sons. Because of YOU, a mother had to bury her daughter! For the love of us, tell me you remember!"

"Her father had displeased me," she said much in the way a woman might recount the most recent meal she cooked.

"Your father and uncle and I had to combine our might to protect you from Ares after what you did! Do you know *why* I convinced those two to come to your aid? When you stilled the winds to stall the Greek fleet, Ares wanted to tear you limb from limb! You probably heard his outcry: 'Artemis has stopped the greatest war in history over a personal affront!' He kicked one of the support columns in the throne room so far, some of the pieces haven't landed yet!"

"Did this surprise you, uncle? Ares has *always* had a short temper!"

"I interceded for you and convinced Poseidon and Zeus to do the same, because I thought you did it for PEACE! Your older aunts, Hera, Athena, and Aphrodite started the avalanche when they asked the Trojan prince Paris to judge one of them 'The Fairest'. I thought YOU were wise beyond your years, Artemis. I thought you were putting a stop to it. The Trojan War was the worse thing the mortals under us had ever done AND YOU COULD HAVE STOPPED IT!"

"As I said before, I rule over the aspects of mortal lives that do not involve men. Or war. Or their other petty endeavors."

"Then why did Agamemnon warrant such hatred from you? You demanded his daughter's blood as compensation for a slain ANIMAL!"

"As I said, he displeased me."

"You demanded blood as the price for the opportunity to spill more blood."

"That I did. Settle down, uncle. She's not even dead!"

"Then who have I had shuffling around down here for the last twenty-three years?"

"A fake. I substituted a stag in her place at the last second. She's an immortal companion of mine now."

"Why? Why bother with such a deception?"

"To maintain the fear and respect of mortals, I had to be as ruthless as father. Or at least *appear* to be. I didn't actually let her die."

"Did it occur to you to inform her *mother* of that development?"

"The Fates showed me what would happen if I allowed her to think that. She stabbed Agamemnon more times than most soldiers would stab an enemy."

"You make a good point there. Agamemnon is one of the mortals I intend to punish. The man ravaged an entire nation to avenge his brother's failed marriage."

"Would Agamemnon have been so eager to storm the Trojan palace if not for Priam's immense store of treasure?" Artemis asked.

"Another good point. Well, Artemis, I will hold you blameless for the carnage if you can justify one of the last results. Troy burned but Trojan children were still born afterwards."

"How can that be?"

"As the invading Greeks poured into Troy, they abandoned all restraint.

They killed Trojan soldiers with an efficiency that made Ares cry tears of joy. They tore the men apart with swords, spears, and arrows. They reserved their most destructive weapon for the Trojan *women*. The one weapon that could penetrate you the same as it could a mortal woman. Then they tore them up the same as the men."

"They were spared the pain of childbirth then," Artemis said matter-of-factly.

"Yes, *they* were. *Those* were the lucky ones. Childbirth is painful for them even when children are what they want most in life. Most of the women of Troy to survive the destruction were carried off to slavery on foreign shores. They had to give birth to children conceived by rape, Artemis," Hades stated that last fact in the same manner as someone telling a man in the hospital that he had driven drunk and killed someone the night before; he didn't intend to, but his lack of consideration had brought never ending suffering on innocent people.

The color drained out of Artemis' face. She took the side of Troy mostly out of solidarity with her twin brother Apollo, the two always took the same side in any given conflict. She was believed to have had a man torn to shreds for trying to violate her or even merely looking at her yet gave her approval for a series of events that led to far more.

"I once sought to protect women from men, yet I conducted myself the same as them. All I could think of was my own pride. I failed those who believed in me. Even we can't turn back time, Hades."

"No, Artemis, we can't. I will find a way to make right what we allowed to go wrong. You and Odysseus both have surprised me. I expected you would react much the way Apollo might. You have placated my wrath. I expected you would be as remorseless as Achilles for your behavior. Go back to your woods, for now. I'm sure we will meet again later."

CHAPTER NINE

THE JUDGMENT OF HADES

"There can be no progress without head on confrontation."
-Christopher Hitchens, English-American author

A thena, Hera, and Aphrodite stepped into Hades' throne room with all the eagerness of people invited to the home of an eccentric relative. The Underworld was a stark contrast to the palace on Mount Olympus where they spent most of their time. Although they were immune to the effects it usually had on humans, it was cold, dark, and dreary enough to chill the soul of even a deity. Nevertheless, the feast laid out on the table gave the place some of the air of comfort they were used to.

"Aphrodite, where are your manners? Even here we don't sit down without our hostess present," Hera said with the tone of a parent telling a child to take their shoes off indoors.

"Sorry, *mother*," Aphrodite replied as a teenager would being told not to stay out late.

Athena, goddess of wisdom and strategy, surveyed the room as a military commander would a battlefield. She was usually the most careful and calculated of the Olympians. It struck her as odd that Persephone would invite the three of them here but not greet them. Her mother and sister seemed too self-absorbed to even notice.

"Something is off here. Persephone invited us here because she's feeling isolated and having marital trouble. Why would she invite *me*? Everyone knows I've sworn off men in general."

Aphrodite responded, "She invited me and mom. Maybe she didn't want you to feel snubbed."

Athena didn't have to wonder for much longer. Persephone and Hades soon entered together, both casting grim expressions. They gave off looks like Hector did when Paris told him he was bringing Helen home with them. Hera saw this and felt what she usually did when learning of one of Zeus' extra-marital affairs. Athena and Aphrodite looked equally perplexed and annoyed.

"Persephone, what is *he* doing here?" Hera asked.

"You do remember that this is *his* domain, don't you? I'm sorry for the deception but it was necessary to get you all down here. *He* wanted to meet with you, not me. To be honest, *both* of us are so enraged at you that we couldn't handle meeting with you separately."

"What did *we* do?" asked Aphrodite in the tone of an oblivious person wondering why anyone would have an issue with them.

Hades held up an exquisitely beautiful golden apple. The faces of all three goddesses lit up like children at the sight of a newly opened candy store. Hades' fingers began to tighten, and the apple started to crack. His fellow Olympians often acted cavalierly, but now his patience was nearly exhausted. The Trojan War had turned him into an angrier man than he'd ever been before.

"You three *really* don't remember it do you? At the wedding celebration of Peleus and Thetis, Eris, goddess of discord, was rather bitter about not being invited. She showed up anyway and threw this apple in your general direction. The inscription reads 'to the fairest'. All three of you thought it referred to you. You asked Zeus to settle your dispute but even *he* didn't want to get involved. He passed the responsibility on to Paris. Please don't tell me you've forgotten who *he* was."

"Wasn't he the guy who Helen had an affair with?" asked Aphrodite.

"Oh, that's *one* way of putting it, Aphrodite. After Paris convinced all three of you to take your clothes off so he could render an informed opinion, you each resorted to bribery. Hera, *you* offered to make him *King* of Europe and Asia; Athena, you offered wisdom and skill in war, and Aphrodite, you offered him Helen of Sparta."

"Helen of Sparta? I thought she was Helen of Troy."

"She BECAME Helen of Troy after Paris accepted your offer! Do any of you have any idea how much carnage resulted from your petty rivalry?"

"The Greeks had been eyeing Troy like a beautiful woman any way," retorted Athena.

"Persephone, why are you participating in this charade anyway? Weren't you kidnapped just like Helen?"

"Not quite like Helen. I was a willing accomplice to Hades' plan. The kidnapping part is technically true; my mother was rather upset about it, hence the whole drowning Earth in perpetual winter until I was returned thing. I had been looking for a way to get away from her for quite a while. Hades was actually nicer than most of the men I'd met. Everyone believed I was totally unwilling because after all, who'd want to be married to the god of the Underworld? I didn't want to be forced to return to mother permanently, so I ate the fruit of the Underworld. He's a much better husband than yours, Hera. I've never caught him shape shifting and sneaking into the bedroom of any mortal women, at least."

Hera glared at Persephone with the same anger she felt when she learned her snakes had failed to kill baby Hercules. Zeus' infidelity was an open secret, but it was still galling to hear anyone discuss it so casually, let alone someone not a core member of the pantheon. Hades looked at her like a judge would an unremorseful defendant. His eyes conveyed to Hera that it would be unwise to respond to Persephone the way she would like to. Persephone looked back at him, appreciative, but obviously wanting to continue.

"As for the other part of your question, Hera, I didn't always care that much about what any of you did. Since I moved to the Underworld, I've helped the ferryman, Charon, bring dead children here. They usually won't get in the boat. Then, with the Trojan War, I had to assist him far more frequently. Have any of you ever seen a baby burned beyond recognition? It looks like a lump of volcanic rock with stumps attached that vaguely resemble human limbs. Or how about a young boy with his rib cage split open by a sword? Those blades are intended to puncture fully grown men. When they hit boys, it's like Ares himself wielded them. Did any of you think for a single moment what would happen if Paris accepted your offer?"

Hera's face replied with a "how dare you question my actions" look before saying, "We don't have to listen to this. Come along Athena, Aphrodite."

Hades' eyes burned as white hot as one of Zeus' lightning bolts.

"YES, YOU DO. NOW SIT DOWN, ALL OF YOU!"

"And what will you do if we don't?"

Hades projected an image from Artemis' recent visit. The lady Olympians were shocked to see the usually gentle giant Cerberus sneak up on Artemis and pin her to the ground.

"Let me remind you of the balance of power. I'm invulnerable here. In the Underworld, even Zeus and Poseidon are powerless against me. At sea, Poseidon can't be harmed by even me or Zeus. And in the sky, Zeus is unbeatable. In our respective domains, even the other eleven Olympians combined can't touch us. There are only three of you. You saw what my guard beast was able to do to Artemis, and she knows how to fight. Two of you do not. So, just imagine what I can do to you. Remember: you're immortal. You're immune to death but not to pain."

All three sat back down as though their legs were suddenly unable to hold them up. Hera felt fear for the first time since the war against the Titans. Aphrodite hadn't felt so exposed since her husband had caught her and Ares in an adulterous encounter and exposed them to the rest. Athena had never felt anything like it before. Her powers of wisdom told her there was no way around this predicament.

"All three of you make me sick. I brought you here together because I can't stomach the idea of bringing you down here separately. Your petty rivalry led to the biggest mass migration to my realm ever. And that's even without counting your individual conduct before that. Aphrodite, you are the least to blame—in *that* context. The worst thing *you* did was cheat on your spouse. And the embarrassment when Hephaestus caught you in the net with Ares—punishment enough. Hera and Athena, I'm considering putting you two into that Brazen Bull instrument."

"Alright then, Hades. Out with it. Just what did we do that was so horrible?" asked Hera.

"Hercules," Hades said with the same tone a genocide survivor might use when speaking of the responsible regime.

"One of my husband's bastard children? You'll have to refresh my memory—he sired enough of them to drink rivers dry," Hera said.

"The one who had super-human strength. Is that specific enough for you? Alright, did you send poisonous snakes after the other ones while they slept in their cribs? Are you not the goddess of women, marriage, family and childbirth? You tried to kill a child!"

"I could not retaliate against Zeus. As you said, even eleven of us combined can't harm him at Olympus. So, I had to strike at his bastard son." This explanation only angered Hades further.

"Did you forget the failed rebellion against him? You managed to chain him up in his sleep, until his old allies from the Titan War came to his rescue, you had him beat. Or you could have lured him elsewhere, the way I got the three of you down here! That's not even the worst part. You couldn't accept that your plan failed after he killed the snakes. YOU DROVE HIM INTO A MADNESS WHERE HE KILLED HIS WIFE AND CHILDREN! MORTALS SHOULD FEAR YOU MORE THAN THEY DO ME! AND YET, FUTURE TELLINGS OF THE STORY WILL FRAME IT AS HIS FAULT! Answer me honestly, Hera. Have you felt even a twinge of regret? A second thought? An ounce of remorse?"

Hera responded faster than a mortal woman would even be able to form a thought.

"No."

"You know, I don't think I'll place you in the Brazen Bull after all. Hercules, go ahead."

Before Hera could even wonder why Hades was speaking to Hercules, she felt a pull on the back of her hair like what she normally found pleasurable. The next sensation was anything but. The external force pulled backward then thrust her face directly into the table in front of her. The force of the impact knocked her backwards, face down on the floor. She had what mortals often described as an "out of body" experience, as though her spirit had been knocked out of her body.

The mother goddess' vision became blurry as she struggled to her feet. She didn't have to complete the task. A firm hand gripped her around the neck and hoisted her off the ground. A mortal woman would have died instantly from the force. Her eyes soon met the most fiery ones she had ever seen. It instantly became clear why Hades spoke to Hercules: he was in the room with them, standing right behind her. Evidently, the demigod known for his brute strength could also sneak around like a sniper.

"Unlike the beasts you fought during your twelve labors, *this* one can not die, Hercules. There's no point in trying to strangle her to death. Not that it's undeserved."

Hades' words registered with Hercules like an order to change direction during a military march. Hercules lowered his arm down, then rapidly up and backward, spiking Hera to the ground like a quarterback would a football. He then walked backwards, sprinted forward, and kicked Hera square in the stomach. The force of the demigod's foot propelled her into the nearest wall with an impact that would have paralyzed a cyclops.

"I'd condemn you to Tartarus if I could, Hera. This will have to do. Don't forget her legs, Hercules."

Hercules pulled from his back the club he used in his twelve labors and brought it down like a divine strike on Hera's legs. The screaming chilled even the most hardened warriors in the Underworld. It was beyond the pain ever suffered by any mortal, even the ones placed in the Brazen Bull. After all, they at least had the mercy of death bestowed upon them. Hercules felt a feeling of relief, like Atlas would were he ever released from carrying the world on his shoulders. Persephone walked over and knelt at Hera's side.

"That, Hera, was for Hercules' children. And all the children of Troy I had to shepherd in here because of what you did. If you could have confined your revenge to Hercules himself, we could understand. Unlike the Trojan War, that massacre was solely because of *you*. I hope you'll remember this the next time you get angry."

Hades looked on with grim and reluctant satisfaction. "I hope you'll be wise enough to listen to my wife, Hera. Hermes, I have need of your services." The messenger god appeared instantaneously. "Take her back to Olympus. I have successfully shown her the error of her ways."

With that, Hermes picked up Hera and fluttered the wings on his sandals. He flew away with the goddess screaming loud enough to destroy a mortal man's eardrums and some of the less robust buildings on the surface. It was heard in distant parts of the world and inspired stories in other mythologies. Hades turned his gaze towards Athena.

"Now, for you, Athena. You participated in that cursed contest with the other two. You also have blood on your hands from before that. It is time for you to answer for Medusa."

"She was raped by Poseidon. I couldn't do anything to him. You and Zeus were both believed to be rapists and…"

"Believed to be?"

"As Hera said, Zeus sired enough illegitimate children to drink rivers dry. Poseidon's total is probably close. Even if you account for the possibility that the numbers have been embellished, I can't believe all his partners were consenting. Either way, his powers make true consent difficult to believe. Zeus was able to force Poseidon and Apollo to build the walls of Troy. He can flatten cities on a whim. How could any woman feel truly able to refuse him?"

"And me?"

"None of us heard your side of the story with Persephone. Zeus was so preoccupied with making sure her mother didn't withhold the coming of spring and harvest indefinitely, no one thought to ask for your side of the story. Demeter convinced all of us that her daughter couldn't possibly want to stay down here with you. We were too willing to believe her."

"And how did this effect how you dealt with Medusa?"

"As you reminded Hera, it took an alliance of several gods combined to briefly overthrow Zeus. I knew the only way to punish Poseidon would be to gain the backing of you and Zeus at a minimum. Sexual assault is something women almost never fully recover from. It's even worse when it's done by one of the gods. Medusa was crippled emotionally. She reminded me of the mindless dead I'd seen down here."

Hades reacted the way a mortal man might upon coming home to find his home destroyed and family murdered. After Hermes informed him of Perseus dropping Medusa's severed head at Athena's altar, he was determined that *other* heads should be chopped off as well. He had jumped to a conclusion about Athena the same as everyone usually did about him. Before he could dismiss her though, he knew there was more to the story. He silently composed himself and then looked at Athena as though telling her to continue.

"I wanted to keep her in my service, Hades. She was an empty shell. The only time she showed any energy was when she thought she was in danger. The only way to heal her was to remove her humanity. The emotional devastation destroyed her beauty before I turned her into a Gorgon. I didn't want to put her in what amounted to solitary confinement, but with her new power to turn people to stone, I couldn't let her near innocents either. This way, she'd be safe from it ever happening again."

"The souls of humans turned to stone still make the journey here after death, Athena. I was confused for a while. When warriors fall in battle, they are seldom the only casualty. Medusa killed so many of them that came after her one at a time. When I receive fallen soldiers, they are usually followed by some of their enemies. Even Ares had no idea what could possibly kill so many fighting men this way."

"I wanted to let her remain on that island relatively undisturbed. I eventually informed Ares. He agreed if they were foolish enough to undertake such a mission, without even consulting him or I, then they deserved what ever happened. We eventually reached a tipping point. The number of fatherless children and vulnerable widows became problematic."

"Your endeavor to protect Medusa from further harm led to a need to protect other people from her."

"Yes. Perseus was the first warrior I found to be worthy. Many of the warriors who became her stone garden wanted personal glory. Others were worse. Several guessed correctly that her eyes could turn people to stone even if her head weren't attached to her body. The Fates told me humans would one day create new words for what such a thing could do: weapon of mass destruction. Even Ares agreed someone had to be helped to kill Medusa. In the wrong hands, her head could end warfare—and humanity itself."

"Why was Perseus found to be worthy?"

"His motives were pure and selfless. All he wanted to do was neutralize the man who wanted to posses his mother. He was the first man to undertake the quest who wouldn't misuse the power he would acquire. It was a joint effort between me, Hermes, Ares, and Hephaestus. We made sure Perseus had what he needed to succeed."

"I'm sorry, Athena. I would have intervened if you had asked. I understand why you didn't. Do you still have the head?"

"I do."

"Bring it to me. I will send Charon and Hermes to recover the rest of her remains. Her soul made it here somehow. If anything can be done, we will do it. I have previously allowed mortals to rejoin the living. If we can restore Medusa, I will allow her to do the same. Before this conversation,

I had my mind set on retribution. All I thought of was making my fellow Olympians feel the pain they caused. I must also pursue justice."

"My heart has been wounded ever since. I can't tell you how much I regretted supporting the Greeks in the war Hades. I failed to protect one of my acolytes in my own temple. I favored Odysseus so much because he was a thinking man. I was so proud of him when he thought of the horse. I never considered what he would do afterwards. I failed to foresee that all those women would be taken back to Greece as trophies. When Ajax the Lesser raped Cassandra while she sought refuge in my temple, my hands weren't tied like they were with Poseidon. I withdrew my support for the Greeks immediately. The next morning, I convinced Poseidon to do the same. I helped Odysseus home after the war to protect his wife Penelope. After Poseidon punished him for blinding the cyclops, I knew Penelope would be vulnerable. I couldn't counteract Poseidon, but I could protect Odysseus. I gave Penelope the idea to stall the suitors with the burial shroud. I considered killing them myself but I saw what happened when we interfered with mortals too much."

Hades looked at Athena like a father whose daughter had just buried her husband. His urge to punish her had been destroyed just like Troy. Her sorrow moved him perhaps even more than Artemis had.

"Athena, you are wiser than any other, divine or mortal. That is what the mortals call a double-edged sword. Your cleverness means your mistakes are proportionally larger. I do not know how to make this right. It would help me to have your wisdom to draw from. Will you join me?"

"Yes. We can't continue like this, Hades."

Hades embraced her like a father welcoming home a prodigal son (or daughter). The warmth given off spread through the Underworld and restored some of the spark of the living to its occupants. It radiated out into the world of the living and fertilized crops, pacified violent men, and for a short time, no mortal in Greece died. Some of the balance of the universe had been restored when the two of them reconciled.

Aphrodite had sat there in silence while Athena had defended herself. The goddess of love and beauty had lost the haughty expression she entered Hades' domain with. Before Hades could even ask her to speak, she sprang to her feet.

"Helen was miserable. She had been forced to marry a man the same age as her father! I couldn't allow it to continue—she prayed to several of us for deliverance, Hades. I offered her to Paris because I was planning to rescue her from Menelaus and Sparta anyway."

"I understand your inclination, Aphrodite. You did not understand or even consider the ripple effect. Did you have any idea you would incite a massive war? The mortals call her 'The face that launched a thousand ships.' You should have been more discreet. Whether Helen was willing or not, you used her as *currency*. You reduced her to a bargaining chip. We're above the mortals but you must not reduce them further. Will you join me in restoring justice? Athena and Artemis are already onboard."

"I will."

Hades smiled like a man who had just experienced a rare incident of good fortune. He did not know what would be necessary to heal the Greek world but having two more Olympians commit to the cause gave him hope. At the very least, they would help stop the bleeding. He knew there was much to do, and suddenly remembered that it wasn't *all* the gods' fault. After all, mortals had still wreaked so much unnecessary destruction. Hades could not allow *them* to go unpunished either.

CHAPTER TEN

AGAMEMNON FACES
A HIGHER POWER

"Older men declare war. But it is the youth that must fight and die."
-Herbert Hoover, President of the United States

Hades sat in this throne room with a cautious feeling of optimism. His fellow Olympians had shown far more remorse than he expected of them. It had not escaped his notice that he had only confronted the women so far. Of the younger ones, only Apollo and Ares remained. Hermes and Hephaestus had done nothing to incur his wrath. A few mortals had so far not faced his judgement, and of course, he would have to face the other two of the "big three"—Zeus and Poseidon.

"Persephone, join me!"

Persephone entered nervously. Although she fully supported her husband's quest for justice, she was a bit traumatized from watching the recent confrontation.

"Of course, my love. Whose feet shall we hold to the fire next?" she asked.

"Agamemnon, of course. I doubt he will have answers satisfactory to explain his conduct, but then, I did not expect Odysseus would either. Depending on how he responds, I might summon Menelaus as well."

"That might prove a little difficult. Menelaus still lives. He and Helen rule over Sparta."

"I will have to wait until they arrive here to pass judgment. Charon told me what happened when he and Hector arrived in Ithaca. Their mere presence there was a disturbance against nature. It was only because of the severity of Odysseus' crimes that killing him did not destroy the kingdom. I have absolute power over the dead, balanced by a lack of power over the living."

"Of course. Hades, I, I don't know about this. What Hercules did to Hera..." Persephone started.

"Was unfortunately necessary. I know it was brutal, Persephone. Do you know why I let Artemis, Athena, and Aphrodite leave here unharmed?" Hades interrupted.

Persephone's face pleaded for him to elaborate, desperately hoping his answer would alleviate her fears.

"Because of what I saw on their faces. In their eyes, I could tell that I had gotten through to them. Remember, my family and I are immortal. When they are down here, I can inflict pain on them or even dismember them, but they will eventually recover. I wanted them to feel the guilt Hercules did. That will restrain their future actions more effectively than any threat ever could."

"I understand, but I didn't think it was possible to do what he did to her."

"It usually is not, but remember, Hercules is a son of Zeus, imbued with super strength. I granted him more for a short time. You're handling this exactly as you should. The mortals who control things on Earth—do you think they feel guilt about what they do? Most soldiers are haunted by what they do in war, but those that send them to war care not about the havoc they create. Ares tells me the Fates have shown him it will get worse. It is currently the custom that when nations go to war their kings usually lead them. That practice will eventually cease."

"You make good points. Unlike most mortal royalty, I have held charred, dead, and dismembered children in my hands. If they saw the results of their machinations up close and personal, they might be more restrained. Let's bring him in now."

"I instructed Charon to bring him here exactly when we were ready."

With that, Charon escorted the late Mycenean king into the throne room. Agamemnon still wore the attire of a king but not the bearing. The Underworld had a way of draining the spirit of most of its residents. Most did nothing but shuffle aimlessly around the cold, dreary cave-like environment. Royalty tended to retain their personalities for longer. Hades was still confident that his efforts would bring part of Agamemnon back to life so he could answer for what he had done.

"Hello, Agamemnon. King of the Myceneans, commander of the Greek invasion force of the Trojan War. Tell me, why did you do it?"

"To return my brother's wife Helen to Sparta where she belonged."

"Oh yes, Helen. The 'face that launched a thousand ships'. Tell me, Agamemnon, was it really *that* many?"

"It might have been," Agamemnon replied with an apathetic affect, trying to project a tone that the Trojan War was just a typical Tuesday for him.

"It *might* have been? How do you not know? Surely a military leader of your proficiency would have known exactly what assets he had under his control," Hades pushed.

"A thousand ships—you know we mortals tend to embellish things. What is the point of this questioning, Hades?" he replied with the tone of a man not used to having to explain himself.

"I wanted to see how much you remember. Embellished or not it still sounds…. Excessive."

"What do you mean?"

"A thousand ships to retrieve *one woman*. Did you even process that fact at the time?"

"The abduction of Helen was an affront not just to Sparta but all of Greece! We would have been the laughingstock of the world had we not reacted accordingly! It figures *you* would have a problem with retaliation for kidnapping, Hades. Isn't that how you met *your* wife? I understand why you did though. She's a fine piece of…."

Persephone kneed Agamemnon in the stomach before he could finish. The restoration of some of his spirit had also restored his reflexes, for he instantaneously bent forward at the waist the way a living man would from the same blow. She grabbed the back of his hair with both hands, pushed his head away from her and then pulled it back towards her as her knee rose to connect with his chin. Had Agamemnon been a mortal man, the blows would have rendered him paraplegic.

"I was not a victim of Hades! It was staged as a kidnapping but I was in on it! My mother was so overbearing.... I knew he was interested in me. I figured I could do worse, and that there would be perks to being married to a god. I was right about both, but I found he was such a better husband than I ever could have expected. You mortal men could learn a thing or two from him. I have a revelation for you: things will go much better for you if you don't treat your wives like property!"

"I think he gets your point, Persephone."

Agamemnon staggered to his feet. He couldn't believe any woman, mortal or otherwise could possibly strike with such force. After all, women were supposed to be seen and not heard. They weren't supposed to participate in the business of men. Their duty was to remain at home, loyal and chaste, whether their men were lowly peasants or mighty rulers. From his perspective, a woman's place was wherever her husband wanted her to be.

"You're lucky I stopped her, Agamemnon. I've restored your life functions just enough for you to feel pain. I hope you've gathered that since you're here, you've died, thus you can't die again. Therefore, any pain inflicted upon you won't be ended with death. I am all powerful within this realm, more so after the influx of new arrivals you sent me. I can endow anyone I please with such strength. To put it simply, my wife is as strong as Achilles when she's in our home. You would do well to speak to her respectfully. Now, why so much effort to bring Helen back?"

"When Helen's father was marrying her off, everyone was afraid of being a target. An agreement was reached that whoever did not win Helen's hand would assist the winner in getting her back should the need arise. It was necessary to keep the peace."

"That explains how you were able to assemble such a massive force. But tell me, was helping your brother get revenge really on your mind as you crossed the Med?"

"Of course!" Agamemnon responded.

"It was quite convenient then that she had been abducted to a palace with the world's largest store of treasure and plunder, was it not?"

"I admit, that was a happy coincidence."

"I saw your face when your brother was finally reunited with her. You had very little reaction. When you reached Priam's treasure store, though…. I hadn't seen happiness like that since Zeus rescued the rest of us from Chronos' stomach. Theseus came close when he escaped the labyrinth."

"Alright, yes, I was mainly driven by avarice. I had had my eye on Troy for quite a while anyway. The abduction of Helen was just an excuse."

"An excuse. Tell that to *them*."

Hades turned around and gestured for Agamemnon to turn around and look behind him. The throne room had suddenly expanded to many times it's normal size. Dead Trojans occupied all of it. All appeared as they would have looked after a violent death. Some had dead vacant eyes, others had an obvious craving for blood.

"I do not hold the death of men like Hector against you. I've met many warriors over the years, Agamemnon. Some of them dedicate their lives to war, never wanting before or after to do anything else. Others pick up a weapon only during times of great need and hope desperately to live long enough to put it down. But it wasn't enough for you to kill all of them, was it? You had to send most of the women and children here too, didn't you?"

"That's how it is, Hades. Empires expand by war. It has been so since the beginning of time and will remain so as long as men walk the earth."

"I shouldn't have been too surprised. After all, you had no problem killing your own daughter. I'm sure you never thought of Iphigenia again after you landed at Troy, did you?"

"I had a war to fight."

"You were discreet about it though. You sent a messenger to your palace to order your wife to bring her to Paulus to be married off. Why did you not simply order your wife to kill her?"

"She never would have complied. The goddess Artemis said I had to do it personally."

"I've had her called down here to answer for that as well. I think I'll let *her* tell you."

Agamemnon then felt a blunt strike from behind. This one knocked him to the ground faster than the knee strikes from Persephone. His head recovered faster, as though it was meant to only stun him briefly and not fully knock him out. He made it to his feet and saw the goddess of the hunt in front of him once again, with the same fire she had when they met all those years ago.

"That was for Iphigenia. The reason I avoid men is men like YOU, Agamemnon! You let your daughter believe she was to be married off to a much older man before you then slit her throat."

"That was at *your* order as the price for the wind…."

Artemis wielded her bow as a quarterstaff and struck him in the rib cage. Two of his ribs broke and pierced his heart. The same blow to a living man would have triggered a slow fatality, at least with the primitive battlefield medicine of the time. She glared at him with the same hatred Hera usually had for Zeus' illegitimate children.

"I should have at least told your wife what really happened. You didn't kill her. I switched her out for a stag at the last possible moment. She's been living with me ever since. You didn't even fight for her. You didn't try to bargain. Then, after burning Troy, you took home a girl not much older than she was to use as an outlet for your carnal desires. You remember the Trojan priestess, Cassandra, don't you? Your wife killed Cassandra shortly after you. It was good to see you did not get to place your evil hands on EVERYTHING you wanted to touch!"

Agamemnon continued to show no remorse. He had the same demeanor he usually had in his strategy meetings with his fellow warrior kings on the shores of Troy. Hades agreed with Artemis' sentiments and interjected.

"All those people dead because of your greed, great Agamemnon. Troy was built over the span of centuries and destroyed in a span of hours. Yes, there was the ten-year long war but even ten years is the blink of an eye on that scale. You were already a wealthy and powerful man. Because of you, so many Greek children grew up fatherless. Many of the ones born after your fleet sailed are fathers now, having no idea how to *be* fathers because you threw theirs into a meat grinder. So many Trojan women and children carted off to slavery in Greece. All those women reduced to nothing but outlets for men's lust because of YOUR GREED! All that bloodshed just so men like you, who already had more than anyone else, could have MORE. Trojans—dispense justice!"

With that, the crowd surrounding Agamemnon encircled him like a pack of lions cornering their next meal. He let out a scream of pure terror.

The King of the Myceneans had believed himself to be untouchable. This incident would be worse than his mortal death. The stabs from his wife Clytemnestra had finished him before his mind could register what was happening. Without death being possible here, he would feel every single strike.

"Persephone, Artemis, when the Trojans finish with him, place him inside the Brazen Bull. If any mortal man deserves that fate, it's him."

CHAPTER ELEVEN

THE INDICTMENT OF APOLLO

"Just as ripples spread out when a single pebble is dropped into water, the actions of individuals can have far-reaching effects."
-Dalai Lama, Tibetan Buddhist spiritual teacher

Deceased people shuffled aimlessly through the Underworld, as usual. The new arrivals still bore their causes of death. The signs of whatever had killed them would eventually fade with time. Whatever sent them there, they were all equal upon arrival. Regardless of their path in life, everyone from king on down would eventually reach the same destination.

Hades paced through his domain, looking upon the mortals now under his care. Until the Trojan War, he had not considered whether such an arrangement was fair and just. On his left, passed a Greek soldier who had taken home severed limbs as trophies. On his right, passed a kind and generous family man. He asked himself why he was allowing (or forcing) those two men to occupy the same space.

Things were not entirely going wrong for him, however. Persephone had been happier lately—it had been a while since she had to accompany Charon. Agamemnon was now paying for having sent so many people there. The lord of the dead knew he still had much to do to balance the scales. He had begun to think about his next move while making his way to the throne room. This proved unnecessary.

"Hades, we need to talk!"

Hades was rarely surprised, but it still happened from time to time. This was one of those times as he now saw the sun god Apollo visiting his realm. Apollo was not usually this reserved or polite. He was minding his manners because of Hades being so powerful in his own realm. The normally hot-headed twin brother of Artemis had the demeanor of a desperate man interceding to save someone he cared about. The previous Olympians had arrived with much different attitudes.

"What can I do for you, Apollo?"

"What did you do to my sister? She hasn't been herself since her recent visit here."

"I merely made Artemis feel something we gods have felt far too little: pain."

"I don't understand."

"Of course you don't, Apollo. For too long, we have ruled and judged from a distance. We have intervened when it suits our fancy. This selective intervention has magnified the damage human beings have inflicted on themselves and each other."

"Yes, but how does that concern Artemis specifically?"

"Each of us rules over an aspect of human life, Apollo. I made her realize what *she* had done, to put it simply, she failed to stop the war."

"The Trojan War was set in motion with the abduction of Helen. Artemis had nothing to do with that."

"Nothing to do with *that*. However, she decided to get involved after Agamemnon offended her. She stilled the winds needed to take the Greek invasion force to Troy."

"And she restored them when the price was paid. I'm sorry, Hades, but I still don't see the problem here."

"The problem, Apollo, was that she had an opportunity to stop the madness and did not. I'm glad you're here, though—you are on my list as well."

"Why me?"

"Cassandra."

"Who is Cassandra?"

"You really don't remember, do you? She was a Trojan princess. She promised to return your love in exchange for the gift of prophecy. You agreed, then she backed out. You retaliated by cursing her with never being believed. I know you could populate a small country with your sex partners but please tell me this description narrows it down for you."

"Oh yes, her. What can I say? I had to send a message about what happens to people who offend the gods."

"You had to send a message. Funny you should say that—Artemis said something similar. You two do tend to stick together."

"We're twins, uncle-a package deal."

"You both had opportunities to prevent or mitigate the war. Tell me, did you even once consider the ripple effect of what you did to that woman?"

"No."

"She foretold correctly that Troy would burn. Had you not done what you did, Troy might have been better prepared. You strongly favored the Trojans, didn't you? Yet your interference doomed them. Did she deserve to be taken home as a slave by Agamemnon, Apollo? That's what ultimately happened to her. She was never violated by him though. His wife penetrated them both with a dagger. Many times. By the time Clytemnestra finished with her, she looked like she had been crushed by a cyclops."

"Like I said, she had to pay for what she did." was Apollo's only answer.

"Apollo, you've never fully thought things through. How did her terms not strike you as being suspect? Love is something mortals either feel, or they don't. How could you believe someone who would love you in exchange for a divine gift would have any genuine affection for you? Why did you even give her the gift of prophecy?"

"Ok, Hades, you got me. I just wanted to have sexual relations with her. Is *that* what you want to hear?"

"Not exactly, Apollo. I do like your honesty, but no. You say that like a student giving the answer he thinks will earn him a passing grade. I want you to realize what you did."

"I'm still confused."

"If you wanted to punish Cassandra for what she did, I could understand. As I have said, you made Troy less prepared, and you never think things through. Cassandra had to watch every single person she knew be killed or carried off into slavery. If you had forced her to remain a virgin, that would be one thing, but you made her witness so much death.

She lost her entire family and country and home. Surely you realize how disproportionate that retribution was."

"I admit I didn't intend to punish her immediate family."

"It wasn't just them." Hades held out his hand and projected an image of all the Trojans and some Greeks filing into the Underworld the night that Troy was extinguished forever. Trojan women. Trojan children. Trojans of all ages. All bore signs of arriving there by unnatural means.

"Apollo, did the people of Troy deserve to pay for what she did?"

"It is unfortunate that they had to," Apollo said with a tone indicating his resolve was beginning to waiver. Hades sensed this in him. Apollo's body language had become less relaxed, and he began to show fear, for possibly the first time ever.

"Your sister realized the error of her ways, Apollo. *That* is why she hasn't been herself since I lured her down here. You should recall that shortly before her visit she enlisted your help in chasing down a three-headed beast. I sent Cerberus to get her here. He succeeded. As you've said, you and Artemis are a package deal. Therefore, you are at least partially responsible for each other's actions."

"How so?"

"I said she realized the error of her ways. When she stilled the winds for the Greek fleet, I thought she was stopping the madness. You were the closest to her. Did you think to intercede with her?"

"No. We gods never interfere with each other's individual endeavors."

"For the most part, you are right. Exceptions have occurred. Zeus intervened after I was believed to have abducted Persephone…"

"Believed? It wasn't true?" Apollo looked curious.

"She does actually love me, Apollo. Demeter, Persephone's mother was overbearing, the type humans will later call a 'helicopter parent'. She would never have let her go. We thought she'd get over it soon. Then Demeter withheld the harvest and Zeus said if I didn't return her, all our subjects would die. Zeus wanted to make it a permanent return, so Persephone ate some of the food here so that she'd be bound to return."

"I never heard this version of that incident."

"Of course, you haven't. I've always been believed to be a creepy loner. The version of me as an evil abductor has been too easy to believe. I blame myself and all your elders for setting such a bad example for you. All of us contributed to this calamity, Apollo."

"Yes, Hades, but I likely did the Trojans less harm than good. I did build the walls."

"Only because Zeus forced you to."

"True, but you say my curse on Cassandra doomed the Trojans despite my lack of intent to do so. Therefore, my participation in the rebellion against Zeus *aided* them despite my lack of intent to do so."

"Yes, your actions and their outcomes are ironically opposite sides of the same coins."

"When the daughter of one of my priests was abducted, I sent a plague into the Greek camps. I also killed many Greeks personally. I helped them more by guiding the arrow into Achilles' vulnerable heel than any of their own people did."

"As noble as that is, Apollo, no matter what you did, something terrible happened. How many Greek soldiers would have survived if left to their own prowess? You left many Greek children fatherless. Did they deserve that misfortune more than the Trojan children, or vice versa?"

"So, my involvement gave one side or the other an unfair advantage, or handicap?"

"Yes. You're beginning to see the problem. What should we gods have done differently?"

"We should have protected them better. It was Ares' fault then. He is the god of war, surely *he* drove the mortals to carry out such destruction."

"He was part of the problem, yes. However, I did not plan to bring you down here to discuss *his* actions. I still don't. We're talking about *you*, Apollo. Now, part of what you just said is completely true. Which part do you think I'm talking about? Say it out loud to yourself."

"We should have protected them better." Apollo repeated his previous statement with the realization of someone who knew all their actions had backfired. Hades had penetrated his conscience at last. He had hoped repeating the approach he used with Artemis would work, and that he did not need to endow someone with divine strength to dispense justice. The gravity of Apollo's actions had sunk in.

"I did protect the Trojans, but so many of us protected the Greeks. We cancelled each other out," Apollo offered.

"Yes, we did. We should have steered the mortals away from their base selfish instincts. I don't know how we can install empathy in them. How do you make humans think about the ripple effects, the suffering masses far from them?"

"I do not know," Apollo answered.

"We've never controlled the humans. Oh, we've interacted with them, punished them, rewarded them, fornicated with them but we've never forced them to do anything. I have never admitted it. As far as I know, neither have the rest of us, but I think we have always known that forcing humans to do what's right would be opening another kind of Pandora's Box," Hades said.

"How so?"

"We have the ability to turn up anywhere, anytime. We can stop humanity from doing the horrible things they do to each other, but as soon as we do it that one time, we would then have to do it every time. They would come to resent us and then as soon as we let up, they would behave even worse. They can't be truly virtuous unless it comes from within, or at least kept in check by each other, not us."

"We have interfered too much, haven't we?"

"Yes, I believe we have. I have confronted the Olympians individually. I must later confront them all collectively. It will likely be our most significant meeting since first gathering to battle the Titans. Leave me, Apollo. I must prepare for my meeting with Ares."

CHAPTER TWELVE

THE LAMENTATION OF ARES

"I hate war as only a soldier who has lived it can, only as one
who has seen its brutality, its futility, its stupidity."
-Dwight D. Eisenhower, President of the
United States and General of the Army

Charon rowed his ferry boat across the River Styx with great trepidation. His master Hades had been sending him on unusual assignments lately. First, he had to transport the late Trojan warrior prince, Hector, across the River Styx, across the Med into Ithaca. The hard part was ensuring Hector didn't stay in the mortal world too long. No one knew exactly what disaster would occur in that event and no-one wanted to find out.

Second, he was now tasked with transporting the war god Ares to the Underworld, on the same route he took mortals. For most, he demanded a silver coin for payment. With this passenger, he was afraid to even speak. Mortals often could not even speak in his presence.

Ares stood, stoic and silent. Charon could not believe the embodiment of war, brutality and bloodlust remained as calm as a statue. Their interaction consisted of Ares informing Charon that the lord of the dead had sent for him. As the gods could not die, they could avoid the Underworld

67

for eternity if they wished. Death was unnatural to them and except for Hermes, the boat ride down the river was the most expedient route.

As he entered the Underworld, Ares made a voluntary offering of food to the second most powerful occupant: Cerberus. While Ares remained neutral to Hades (despite the nature of their relationship) he retained great affection for the guard beast. Cerberus ate with great enthusiasm then used his three tongues to register his appreciation on Ares' face. Ares scratched the dog behind all three pairs of ears and continued.

The god of war entered the throne room calmly. Hades watched him enter with relief. He had feared Ares would not be agreeable to meeting him there, after all he had to use deception to get Artemis, Hera, Athena, and Aphrodite to visit. Apollo had only visited out of concern for his sister. As dead mortals, Odysseus and Agamemnon had no choice but to appear at his command.

"Ares, thank you for coming. I hope you found the voyage pleasant."

"I appreciate your concern, Hades, but you know *no one* finds that voyage pleasant. Even we gods don't like to be in Charon's company, and *our* passage in his boat is free."

"*Your* passage is free? As opposed to....?"

"You didn't know? You've been unaware of how the mortals bury their dead with a silver coin to pay him?"

"Why, yes. This is a revelation to me. Death is natural, commerce is not. I did not authorize this practice. I shall have to have a word with Charon."

"Well, please convey my apologies to him. I had always assumed he did this with your blessing. He did let up a bit during the recent war, making allowances for all the battlefield deaths. He may have simply billed the survivors."

"If this is true, then he will join Agamemnon inside the Brazen Bull. Or perhaps something worse. That is a matter for another time. I'm surprised you're so...polite. I'm not exactly your favorite relative."

"You expected I would stampede in here, sword drawn, asking who dares summon the god of war, even when I know it was you?"

"To be honest, yes. You're much calmer than I expected."

"I do talk to Athena, you know. She reminded me that even the other eleven of us *combined* can't harm you down here, and that was even *before* the Trojan War made you more powerful. It made me *less* powerful, believe it or not."

"How is that possible?"

"How effective is Cerberus after eating a large amount?" Ares asked.

"But you thrive on war and death and conflict. You're the reason it exists. You are its creator!"

"No, Hades. I did not create war. War created me."

Hades reacted with the shock of a young adult man learning that the man who raised him his whole life was not his biological father and that he was the product of his mother's extra-marital affair. War filled his domain the way the drug war would later fill prisons. If there was one Olympian whom he wished were mortal, it was Ares. His children were literally named Fear and Terror, after all.

"I absorbed so much from the Trojan War that I've had my fill for a while. That's why I'm so calm and agreeable right now. Hades, your memory is off. You remember me participating in your war against the Titans, don't you? I wasn't there. Oh, I know all about it. My brothers and sisters have recounted the details to me."

"How? This can't be, you're one of the twelve," Hades said.

"I'm almost as old. I emerged when humans first coordinated amongst themselves to attack other groups of humans. Individuals had killed before, of course, but I didn't come to be until they gave their groups names. I don't thrive on murder. I know that's odd to say given that war and murder are often believed to mean the same thing."

"Then how do I remember you being there?"

"Zeus and Hera believed me to be their son. After they figured out where I came from, their feelings did not change. They appointed me god of the physical, untamed aspects of war. They thought I'd make an excellent counterpart to Athena, who represented the thinking parts such as strategy."

"Yet you were on the losing side of the greatest war."

"Yes, Greek intelligence defeated Trojan brute force, or the defensive equivalent of brute force. Apollo and Poseidon built those walls so great, even I couldn't penetrate them. Hades, do not blame me for the Trojan War."

"Why not?"

"As I said, I did not create war. War created me. For the first few years of the war, I was strong enough that I could have defeated Zeus in single combat. The high concentration of fighting men and the size of the battles made me the most formidable force of all of us. Then as the war went on, I lost strength. Both sides lost motivation. Think about it—Athena knew the horse trick would work because the Trojans wanted so bad to believe the war was over."

"You raise good points, Ares, but why should I not blame you for driving men to kill each other?"

"Do you know why you've been so much more powerful than I, aside from being one of the big three? Because death is natural to humanity. War is not. I did not transform peaceful men into killers. They did."

"Which they do you speak of?"

"Men. Also, Demeter."

"How can you blame the goddess of the harvest?" Hades asked.

"Yes, she provides fertility to the land, and to women. She works close in hand with my on again/off again partner, Aphrodite. She does not always provide sufficient harvest."

"Go on."

"Men kill because of the struggle to survive. Have you any idea how hard men work to grow food from the land? With the primitive methods they use, it often kills them, slowly, over decades. War provides an escape—many men have picked up the sword for the sole reason that they wish to put down the plough. At worst, they get a much quicker death. At best, they get glory, a form of immortality."

"How does shortening their lives make them immortal? From the best warriors to the worst, from the highest decorated general to the lowliest foot soldier, they all eventually join me here."

"Immortality among their fellow man. You get visions from the Fates, don't you?"

"I do. I'm guessing you intend to share what they've shown you," Hades responded.

"Oh yes, they've shown me quite a bit. Mostly because war will shape so much of human history. I will one day be even stronger, then face the beginning of my death. They don't know how I will die though."

"You're a god, you can't die."

"War created me. When it goes away, so will I," Ares stated.

"I'm having trouble believing that but go on."

"You have no idea how big the world is, Hades. We gods have stuck to one region so much, we've barely seen any of it. And human weapons will be rather primitive for the time being."

"For the time being.... you've seen worse ones?" Hades asked.

"If by worse you mean deadlier, oh yes. Much more so. Some of humanity's future inventions will render a man unidentifiable upon impact."

Ares projected an image of a slender, bearded, sun tanned man ducking for cover behind a solid built wall of a building that was only partially standing. Hades did not recognize the wood and metal object in his hands but could infer that it was a weapon of some kind. The man held the object around the corner from him and it made noises before he ducked for cover. His head then exploded in a mist of blood and brain matter, followed by a much louder noise.

"You are right, Ares. Even that man's parents wouldn't recognize him after that strike. The noise confused me though. The noise happened *after* the weapon was used."

"Those weapons will use small projectiles called *bullets*. The other warrior fired from so far away that his bullet reached the target before the sound did," Ares explained.

He continued, "And that is only ONE of the many efficient and innovative weapons they will create. There are weapons that fire bullets of that size hundreds of times per minute. *And* those are merely the weapons they use when they can see each other. They'll have others that can simulate *our* power."

Ares showed an image of a large metal bird flying through the sky. It was green and tan colored with oddly shaped claws under its wings, and somehow, a glass window with a human being inside it, located at its head. The bird was adorned with strange markings such as "UH 002", "USAF," and "Gladiator". Then, one of the claws detached itself from under the wing and flew ahead of the bird. Hades could not believe humans would ever be able to build such a thing. Zeus would be proud.

The detached claw flew at great speed towards a mountain. Upon reaching the mountain, the claw seemed to dig a hole and then disappear.

A massive eruption of dirt and rock, not seen since the Titan War, followed. Hades looked as though an ant might, if it could fully understand how much bigger human beings were than it was.

"I suppose they will never again have to infiltrate places like Troy. Even *we* couldn't build something that could withstand that," Hades said.

"Oh yes, sieges will one day be obsolete. However, weapons like this one won't be used against nations or armies, no. One day, the major military powers will spend most of their time fighting much smaller opponents. That man whose head exploded in the earlier projection was not a soldier, at least, not one fighting for a nation. He is something man will label an "insurgent". I do not understand what the term means yet— further study will be required. The man who killed him will be a soldier from one of the more powerful countries."

"Oh my….us. I will likely preside over a much larger domain than I do now."

"That remains to be seen, Hades. The Fates tell me that as humanity develops deadlier weapons, there will be more of them to kill yet they will use the weapons *less* often. Once the nations stop fighting each other, small arms will dominate the battlefield. One day, the major nations will stop fighting each other due to *this* creation."

Ares showed Hades an image of a vaguely mushroom shaped cloud. The thick part was massive enough, it blotted out the sun in the sky. A massive whirlwind of dust, earth, wood, metal and other man-made things flew near ground level at velocities even the swiftest birds could never reach. The flash was so bright it would blind any mortal for the last seconds of his or her life. It was as though someone had conjured several volcanoes in one spot and caused them to erupt simultaneously.

"The nations of the world will develop all manner of ranged weapons that they will hesitate to use on each other for fear of escalating to weapons like that one. That weapon will be so powerful, it will be used only twice, and only then to end a long war between the most powerful nations. I'm told that despite their reluctance to use them, man will develop even more powerful versions of it which can be launched from even further away."

"I suppose one day then, you will be the strongest of all of us, Ares. Zeus, Poseidon and I will come to fear you as man does those weapons," Hades admitted.

"I will become stronger and weaker. There will be many wars bigger than the Trojan War, smaller than that one in the coming centuries and millennia. The killing part of war will become less physical as weapons improve. Most of the courage and stamina will be needed to endure the time between battles. I've been told *that* part of war will never change. However, as the humans make me stronger, they will also begin to kill me."

"How can they possibly do both?"

"Demeter will help them with that. Advances in agriculture and reduction in certain activities will one day make the young populations of the major nations less physically able. In fact, many of their children will be more corpulent than most monarchs. If it advances far enough and long enough, then there might come a day where not a single mortal is physically capable of fighting a war."

"The Elysian Fields will lose their appeal if that happens. What point will be there be to have a realm of happiness and abundance in the Underworld if it's how they live their mortal lives anyway?" Hades asked.

"Yes, the Elysian Fields. It's where the elite and most virtuous go when they die, free from the want and privation that plagues most mortals throughout their lives," Ares said.

"I've begun to loosen the admission criteria. Most of the population of Troy will go there, after they live out an alternate life where the war was averted."

"That is your prerogative as ruler of the dead. Speaking of want and privation, that's what drives most mortals to me. While the earth will one day yield more bounty as man learns to grow from it, many will still hunger. So many men will one day pick up weapons in order to ensure they can eat. Hades, for most men, it is not greed that drives them to fight. It is survival and advancement. Warfare will be a common way for men of humble origins to advance to higher stations in life."

"Perhaps, if they learn to build classless societies, then...." Hades began.

"They will try. They won't get it right. Many men will die in the fight to spread equality. The only thing such a system will distribute evenly is misery," Ares interrupted.

"Humans will build you up while they begin to tear you down?"

"Yes. As they explore the earth, humans will become more aware of humans who are not like them, who do not look like them or think like them. They will develop organized hatred for each other. I won't just gain strength from conflicts between nations, I will grow every time so much as two men attack one man solely for the color of his skin. They won't really hate each other for that though. Mankind has already struggled so much for basic survival that anyone different in anyway is their enemy."

"I think I see what you mean, nephew. Demeter is the key. She must be more generous, or man will have to learn how to please her more effectively. The key to ending war is in ending hunger. If a man can fill his stomach without killing other men to do it, then surely he will prefer to do it that way."

"Yes, I hope so. I have seen war, Hades. I am war and war is me. I do not want to continue but I have no choice. I cannot self-terminate," Ares pleaded.

"You can't—but your followers can. Many of them do. Charon often picks up warriors years after the wars are over."

"I know. I know it more than you ever could. Whenever a mortal picks up a weapon and goes into battle, I gain a permanent window into his or her mind. I see their memories for the rest of their lives," Ares explained.

"Odysseus said something similar."

"Odysseus only had his own memories to look at. His clever mind enabled him to win that fight. He was quite adaptable. Many of the men who go to war will adapt to it so well, nothing else will suit them. Many will travel around selling their skills to the highest bidder. They will be called mercenaries, swords for hire. Most will fall in battle, not caring who they fight for."

"And what memories of theirs do you see?" Hades asked.

"The screams. The sounds of steel weapons colliding with each other. Flesh and organs ripped apart. Heads becoming separated from bodies. Severed arms and legs. Seeing other men take their last breath."

"You have experienced all of their trauma."

"Yes. I've seen the future, remember. Eventually, there will be entire vocations devoted to keeping soldiers alive. As mortals gain a better understanding of their bodies, many more of the wounded will survive. They will return home with limbs missing. Wounds that wound have killed men before. No man alive right now has to live with the memory of having either of his legs ripped away from him."

"I had no idea you were so in touch with their plight, Ares. I expected you would use them for your own ends and then discard them. Have you heard how I'm expanding the eligibility for the Elysian Fields?" Hades asked.

"You mentioned it earlier in this very conversation."

"The war made me realize that it is unjust to hold most mortals in near equal conditions regardless of how they lived. The breaking point was when Persephone showed me Hector's son after he was thrown from the walls of Troy. I think I shall send most of the soldiers I receive into paradise."

"Why *most* of them?"

"I must still consider how they lived when NOT at war. Some will do irredeemable things while at war. Or before, or after. The Greeks who took women home as trophies. The ones who ordered the sacrifice of one of Hecuba's daughter to be the bride of Achilles, in DEATH…. Others will go to war solely to satisfy a desire to kill without facing punishment for it—Tartarus will be a more crowded place."

"It won't be all bad. The Fates also showed me that it will bring out the best in some. Some will enter their nation's service only to avoid its dungeons and will die old as well-respected men. It will turn some criminals into scholars and leaders, admired more for what they did in peace than what they did in war. Many will bring home a new appreciation for life. And that's only on the individual level."

"The individual level—what will happen at the higher level?" Hades asked.

"Innovations made for war will improve life in peace. Tools for navigating the globe for instance. Poseidon will not be prayed to for safe passage—as much. There will be larger versions of that metal bird you saw, without the claws. And the medicine used to keep wounded soldiers alive will benefit civilians as well."

"Will human beings ever try to end war?"

"Yes, they will. Unfortunately, those who benefit from it will most always be more powerful than those who do not. I also saw that one day nations will begin to learn how to care for the men that come home broken, traumatized, wounded, crippled, damaged…."

"Begin to learn?"

"The Fates either can't see far enough ahead to the day they will master it or choose not to tell me. I am grateful they have shared as much as they have with me. I dare not ask them for more," Ares said.

"Ares, I could not be more surprised at your true origin or prouder of how you have handled your role. I will be convening a meeting of all of us soon. I don't know what will come of it, but I know we can't continue like this."

"Thank you, Hades. Oh yes, there is one more thing that will be needed to undo the damage of war. The soldiers themselves. Too many of them will confine themselves to the past, afraid to speak of it for fear that the mere stories will kill anyone who hears them, or that they will be branded weak or cowardly for being affected by them. So many of them will resort to the drink. In battle, men fight not for honor or country but for each other. I will encourage them to bring that approach home with them."

CHAPTER THIRTEEN

POSEIDON CAUGHT
IN A STORM

*"Our actions are like ships which we may watch set out to sea, and
not know when or with what cargo they will return to port."*
—Iris Murdoch, British and Irish novelist

The god of the sea made haste for the Underworld. It had been a
long time since Poseidon had met Hades in person, even at Mount
Olympus. He could not recall when, if ever, he'd met with him in the
land of the dead. Charon transported him across the River Styx despite
Poseidon not needing it. He didn't want to anger Hades here. Poseidon
didn't stop to pet Cerberus like most visitors did and proceeded straight
to the throne room.

"Alright, Hades, what did he do?"

"You're being a bit vague, brother. Which *he* are you referring to?"

It occurred to Poseidon that he hadn't stopped to consider that detail.

"The one you referred to in the note," Poseidon answered.

"What note?"

"You sent Hermes to my palace with a note reading, 'I have your son.
If you wish for him to leave the Underworld unharmed, you will see me
immediately.'"

77

"Oh yes, that. I don't."

"You don't… explain yourself, BROTHER! You summoned me here under false pretenses, didn't you?!"

"That I did, Poseidon. I don't know what's worse—that you immediately believed that your son had incurred my wrath, or that you didn't stop to consider *which* son it referred to. Or that you have enough illegitimate sons that you apparently can't keep track of them. That is, if you ever bothered to in the first place. You probably just use Hermes to communicate with them."

"Enough about my carnal activities, Hades—why am I here?"

"A question that answers itself."

Poseidon produced his trident and pointed it at Hades the way one would an accusing finger, "Answer me or I will gut you like a fish!"

"No, you won't. You forget the balance of power. And I've instructed Cerberus to not let you leave unless I allow it."

Poseidon knew he had the weaker hand here and put away the trident.

"I'm glad you recognize the futility. Now, where to begin…. Caeneus, Demeter, Medusa, Athens…"

"What about them?"

"Your victims."

"Victims?"

"You really are going to make me spell it out for you. Alright, one of those things doesn't belong with the others. Can you tell me which one and why?" Hades asked impatiently.

"Either Caeneus or Athens. Both are cities."

"Incorrect. The correct answer is Athens. Even you can't rape a city, Poseidon."

"You're making even less sense now, Hades," Poseidon replied.

"You're being consistent, at least. If you can't even track your illegitimate children, how can you recall all of your *victims*?"

Poseidon's smug facial expression conveyed he still didn't understand and wouldn't care if he did. Hades decided the indirect route wasn't working. He calmly walked to within arm's length of Poseidon. After a quick smile, he threw a left-hand jab into his throat, then a right hand shot to his rib cage and alternated to a left-hand uppercut to the stomach.

Poseidon bent over at the waist after the impact. Hades brought his right elbow into the back of his head. The impact sent Poseidon face first into the floor. A mortal man receiving the same blow would have had a pool of blood on his face and a lifelong scar on his head. No one had dared challenge him like that since the Titan War.

"Are you beginning to grasp why I tricked you down here? I tried being subtle. It did not work. Let's talk about Medusa, shall we?"

"Who?"

Hades grabbed one of Poseidon's ankles, lifted it up and slammed his knee into the floor. He then wrapped his arm and hand around his ankle and twisted in ways that that part of the body wouldn't normally move. Poseidon's screams equaled the cries of thousands of wounded soldiers on a battlefield.

"Medusa was a priestess of Athena. You raped her in Athena's temple. *You had better remember, now.* I can be even less nice if necessary."

"Yes, I remember now. She was fun. I rather enjoyed the struggle."

"Why?"

"What do you mean, why?"

"WHY DID YOU DO IT?"

"I took one look at her and she struck my fancy. That body of hers was *exquisite*."

"Was it really? Please continue," Hades said sarcastically.

"She looked like she had been handcrafted by Aphrodite herself. I felt that a woman of such beauty taking an oath of virginity HAD TO BE a crime against nature."

"No, what YOU DID was a crime against nature! Mortals pray to us for protection, and you did the very thing they seek protection from!"

"Hades, I might be a god, but I still have the same needs as any man."

"And like most men, you confuse your *needs* with your *wants*. I have never at any time received a man here who perished from sexual deprivation. Ok Poseidon, why do you think I'm talking to you as though you did something wrong there?"

"I suppose you have a point. I shouldn't have helped myself to her without informing Athena."

"You still don't get it, do you? Have you any regard for anyone besides yourself? You showed some on at least one other occasion; I think I know which one you'll say. Tell me about the one time I know of that you were."

"Polyphemus."

"Yes, another one of your bastards. Yours and Zeus' could form large enough factions to fight something the mortals will call a "World War". Refresh my memory—what did you do for Polyphemus?"

"He was a cyclops. The great Odysseus and his Ithacan soldiers trespassed in his home at the beginning of their voyage back from Troy."

"Yes, they did trespass. What else happened?"

"They helped themselves to his food. Then, he ate a few of them. While he was sleeping, they filed his club into a sharp pointed, giant stick and blinded him. Then they hid underneath his sheep when he let them out to graze and escaped on their ships."

"But that wasn't the end of it, was it?"

"No. Polyphemus appealed to me for help, so I made Odysseus' voyage home much longer than it would have been otherwise."

"Why should I be surprised? You handled it exactly as we gods handled things before. You took a bad situation and escalated it. Polyphemus had plenty of food. He had livestock and yet he still consumed men, with the intent to consume more."

"He was just trying to get his food back. Of course, since it was in their stomachs, he had to eat them."

"Was it not their right to escape from the situation?"

"It was natural for them to try, but they should have inferred from what they saw in the cave that it belonged to a cyclops. They knew what they were doing."

"You sound just like Odysseus. I asked him why he felt it necessary to kill a helpless child after they had won the war, and while they had time to think about it. His answer is why he is not with Agamemnon in the Brazen Bull right now or Tartarus for eternity."

"Which was?" Poseidon asked.

"He told me that he had endured ten years of war at that point. He had watched his countrymen fight, bleed, and die. He reminded me that we gods *can't* bleed or die. I had never considered the things mortals have endured that we have not. For that reason I did not order any further punishment for him."

"Hades, this is the way. The powerful do what they want," Poseidon said matter-of-factly.

"I've decided that must not continue. I could go on, but you've already exhausted most of my patience. Since we're discussing your past transgressions, how about the Minotaur?"

"What about the Minotaur?"

"Gods damnit, Poseidon, your inability to even remember your misdeeds is astounding. The King of Crete tried to outsmart you by not sacrificing his finest bull to you. So, you put a spell on his wife to make her lust after it. She put on a costume and fornicated with the bull. Nine months later, she birthed the monstrosity known as the Minotaur. It had the body of a man and the head of a bull."

"Ah yes, I got him good, didn't I?" he laughed.

"Oh, yes. Then he eventually came to use that abomination for a cruel ritual where he forced Athens to send fourteen virgin sacrifices to be eaten. Ironically, one of your other bastard sons (Theseus) put an end to that. Well, I see your mind is set, Poseidon. Please accept my apology for the deception I used to bring you down here. Join me for some wine, will you?"

Poseidon was never one to turn down a drink. The two gods walked to the table and poured themselves large cups. Poseidon raised his glass in a friendly gesture and took a deep gulp. Right after the sweet taste hit his lips, he felt lightheaded, and the room suddenly became blurry. A numbness spread from his neck down and he became reacquainted with Hades' floor.

Sometime later, Poseidon's eyes reopened and he remembered consuming the wine. It must have been potent to knock him out so swiftly. The ground underneath him felt hot and coarse—all sand. After a few steps, his feet suddenly felt wet, and a burst of energy hit him the way coffee drinkers say coffee effects them. As he saw the mountains behind him and the vast stretch of water behind him, he was suddenly surrounded.

"Ah good, you're awake. We didn't think you'd be knocked out that long."

Poseidon recoiled in annoyance at the word "we". He looked around and noticed he was surrounded by Hades, Artemis, Athena, Apollo, and Hercules, all armed. It was the biggest meeting of the gods he'd attended in quite a while, and the second he'd been tricked into. Hades stepped within half an arm's length of him.

"We're on Seriphos. It's the island Athena had to send Medusa to after what you did. You don't have to say you raped her; I know you'll never admit it. You can't see it that way."

Athena walked into his field of vision.

"You traumatized her so bad, I had to remove her humanity. Then to protect humanity from her ability to turn people to stone, I had to bring her here. Her lair is in up that hill over there. One last chance—will you help us set it right?"

"Zeus, Hera!" Poseidon called out.

Hades smiled confidently.

"I'm afraid all of the available Olympians are here. I persuaded Hermes and Dionysus to challenge Zeus to a drinking contest. You know our brother can't be bothered when he's on a bender. The god of wine was quite agreeable to my requests. All I had to say was that I'd like to see Poseidon pass out and wake up hungover on a beach. He didn't even ask why. He just laughed and said, 'You had at me at hungover'. I also mentioned it would be a good idea to add an ingredient that would reduce your strength for a few hours after you woke up."

Hades conjured a live feed image of Mount Olympus. Zeus approached a massive cup and poured a cascade of drink into his mouth. Despite the competitive nature of this meeting, Hermes and Dionysus chanted, "Chug, chug, chug!"

"Hera is still recovering from her encounter with Hercules."

Poseidon reacted like a man would to the news of a good friend losing his virginity.

"Well done, nephew. No better way to get revenge on a woman than bedding her!"

Hercules glared at him like a man would at someone proclaiming they had had relations with his daughter. Hades showed another live feed of Olympus. Hera was shown laying in bed, struggling to breath. Her legs seemed to be regaining function after finishing repairs. Her face was so bruised, she was barely recognizable.

"Ares is now in a polygamous marriage with Aphrodite and Hephaestus. They determined it was simpler than all the sneaking around. The god of war is surprisingly traumatized from everything the *mortals* have done. All three have agreed not to come to your aide. I brought us all out here because a fight in the Underworld could possibly enable the dead to escape. So, what's it going to be, Poseidon?"

Poseidon produced his trident and slammed the business end to the ground. The resulting tremor sent all five of his opponents flying backward. He smirked in satisfaction, certain this one strike would deter them from further action. Apollo and Artemis retaliated with a sudden flurry of arrows to break that illusion for him.

Apollo and Artemis silently formed a strategy to rush Poseidon from both sides. The two had fought together enough to know each other's strengths and methods to coordinate with minimal communication. Apollo leaped forward with his bow raised over his head and brought it down like a battle axe to try and knock out Poseidon. Artemis simultaneously ran to his rear and thrusted her bow towards his back.

Poseidon rotated the blunt end of the trident to his rear and deflected Artemis' incoming strike then thrust the pronged end upward to intercept Apollo's. He ensnared Apollo's bow with the prongs and thrust the blunt end backwards to strike Artemis in the abdomen then thrust the other end forward toward Apollo's neck. The sun god managed to step aside fast enough that the point only grazed his shoulder.

With the trident in both hands, the sea god did a counterclockwise spin and dropped to one knee in order to thrust the forks upward into the area between Artemis' neck and chin. She managed to knock the trident aside with one end of her bow and score a glancing blow to his head with the other.

During this sequence, the other three combatants had recovered from Poseidon's initial strike. While Hades was equal in power to him, Athena and Hercules nearly so, none had recently faced such a fierce opponent. Athena specialized in strategy and thus was rather inexperienced at the physical side of battle. Hercules had fought wild beasts but never a deity. And Hades had not been in a fight since overthrowing the Titans.

Poseidon recovered from the blow fast enough before Artemis could position a blow for another strike. He threw a fist into her kneecap and produced the same impact as a club striking a mortal in the same place. She dropped her bow and dropped her hands to the ground to break a total fall. He sprang to his feet and made another attempt to skewer Apollo but was not fast enough.

Poseidon noticed Hercules recovering and raising his club to charge him. He threw the trident at great speed, close enough for the demigod to feel it coming at him but not close to try and catch it. The resulting impact triggered an avalanche at the top of the mountain behind him. Hercules swung his great club like it were light as a feather at the incoming boulders. The fragments landed in pieces on all the continents.

Athena had started a sprint towards Poseidon with her sword and shield ready to strike but diverted to assist Hercules. She positioned herself behind him and covered his flanks with the shield. This proved most fortunate as even his divinely enhanced reflexes couldn't stop all the incoming rocks. The falling pieces were flung all over the island, forcing everyone to duck, jump, and evade.

As Poseidon drew his trident back to thrust it into Artemis, Apollo attempted to thrust a sword into him. Poseidon pushed the trident downward to parry the sword into the sand. His trident thrust would have skewered Artemis successfully if Hades hadn't managed to converge on them and knock the weapon aside. Hades managed to land a haymaker into his brother's head.

The blow didn't stun the sea god for long. He noticed Hercules and Athena had deflected the avalanche and had set their sights back on him. Poseidon realized the odds were beginning to shift against him and he would need help to turn the tide. He immediately screamed out, "Polyphemus!"

A cyclops promptly emerged from the sea and kicked Hades to the other side of the island. Athena made glances at the cyclops' knees and then back and forth at Artemis and Apollo. Poseidon used his trident to launch himself into the vicinity of Hades' landing. With his other four opponents now otherwise engaged, he could fight his brother one to one.

The twin gods leaped backward to what they considered optimal firing range and fired barrages of arrows into Polyphemus' kneecaps. With his immense size, strength, and divine parentage, he could withstand quite a few but he wasn't immune. The combined impact caused him to drop to one knee before he could reach close range on them. His next instinct was to try and remove the arrows.

Athena thought up a plan and she thought it up quick. She looked at Hercules and pointed at her shield. After he acknowledged it, she thrust it skyward then held it low to the ground. Hercules ran forward, leaped onto the shield and was launched skyward, out of sight. By now, Polyphemus had realized his opponents weren't going to let up after the arrows.

The goddess of wisdom ducked and rolled to avoid a swing from the cyclops' massive club. Knowing the beast still had approximately the same anatomy as humans, she threw her shield into his rib cage with sufficient impact to break multiple ribs, pushing one into his lungs and another into his heart. These combined impacts that held him in place yet further enraged him.

Artemis, Apollo, and Athena drew their swords and surrounded him on three sides. Before Polyphemus could decide which of them to try and kill, Hercules had come back down from the sky and landed a perfect blow downward into his head. The resulting impact to the skull sent a tremor down Polyphemus's spine and caused most of his bones to shatter. All his internal organs exploded, and he collapsed like someone had flipped the OFF switch on him.

On the opposite side of the island, Poseidon wielded his trident like an experienced soldier would a spear. Nothing mattered to him now other than driving the shaft through his prey. Hades managed to sneak up on him and tried to land a killing blow with a sword. He managed to partially wound him before Poseidon stabbed him simultaneously with a trident. The two strikes cancelled each other out and caused the equivalent of paper cuts.

"Still jealous, Hades? I know you wanted the sea or the sky but really, you should be over it by now? You still scored a hotter wife than Zeus or I did. *And* she's not a jealous bitch."

Hades tried once again to stab Poseidon, only for each strike to be deflected. Poseidon made several thrusts with his trident, only to find his brother was surprisingly agile and limber. Although he was in human form, Hades was still a god and could thus bend, dip, twist, and dodge in ways a human spine ordinarily wouldn't allow. He found just enough of an opening to kick Poseidon backwards and bounce him off a few jagged rocks.

"My wife is not a jealous bitch because I don't sneak around behind her back, brother. You and Zeus have sired enough bastard children to populate a city or even country! And this is NOT ABOUT ME INHERITING

THE UNDERWORLD! It's about what you and most of our family have done to FILL IT!"

"Whatever do you mean?"

Hades didn't bother replying. If his previous conversation didn't get through to his brother, nothing would. Having had sufficient time to recharge his trident's strike power, Poseidon slammed it into the rocks beneath him to send another shockwave. Somehow, the impact propelled Hades *uphill* into the support column of the one visible structure nearby. Poseidon carefully made his way up the incline, knowing his brother's allies would be coming for him if Polyphemus hadn't taken care of them.

As soon as he came within eyesight of his target, Poseidon hurled his trident at full speed. Once again, it missed and became embedded in the support column before he could summon it back. The missed attack still emboldened Poseidon, for Hades had run inside to evade him. Oh yes, he thought to himself. His brother had realized the futility of trying to fight him and was running in terror.

Poseidon made his way inside the small building. It appeared to be a smaller version of Athena's temple. The interior was filled with more dimly lit rooms, hallways, and walls than a building of its size should have been able to hold. Its real standout feature, however, was the small army of stone statues. Warriors of all kinds had been petrified with terrified expressions on their faces from the moment of death.

Hades knew *he* had the advantage now. The battle had now shifted to a confined space with a resemblance to his domain. As the ruler of the dead, he had seen more scared faces than any of the other gods, so the faces on the stone soldiers shook him less than they did most. He heard Poseidon making his way through the interior while trying to remain discreet. Hades picked up the faint noises he made with his walk and used them to evade and circle back towards him.

Both gods still began to experience the fear that must have been felt by the unfortunate previous visitors. Neither had experienced the subtle yet harsh smell emanating from the walls and the floor. The fear-based sweat from all the prior combatants had soaked into the walls and urine had been absorbed into the floor, both lingering like ghosts that didn't bother to hide.

Once he had closed to the ideal distance behind him, Hades kicked a statue at Poseidon as hard as possible. The unlucky warrior had been raising a spear up to hurl at his target but it never left his hand. Hades kicked him hoping his stone spear would hit Poseidon's head. His strategy proved creative but unsuccessful.

Poseidon was quick enough to whirl around and guide the three prongs into the statue before it could strike him. He almost wasn't, for the tip of the spear was within arm's length of him before he was able to split it in half. Hades never could have anticipated his next action. Poseidon swung his trident much like a baseball bat and hit the top half of the statue back in his direction. It missed and struck a far wall, shattering into much smaller pieces.

Seeing this attack nearly work inspired Poseidon to repeat the same strike with several other nearby statues. Hades quickly made use of a discarded shield he found on the floor. Not all the previous contestants in this arena had been holding their weapons or equipment when they died. The deflected statues were all reduced to powder from Hades deflecting them into the walls.

Hades charged forward like an angry bull, confident his shield would protect him from subsequent projectiles. It proved redundant as Poseidon did not employ any. Instead, he dropped to one knee and held his trident horizontally with his hands at each end of the pole. The shield rammed into the trident and brought Hades' forward momentum to a halt. The two gods tried to push each other backward, to no avail.

Poseidon was the first to think up a way to break the stalemate. Rising to stand upright, he rotated his whole body and used the momentum to push Hades into a wall. He spun the trident in such a way as to stab Hades in the foot. Then he spun it around and used the other end to deliver a strike to his opposite kneecap. Hades had been brought to his knees.

The struggle was still far from over. Hades shrank himself small enough to cover his entire front with the shield. His legs may have been damaged, but his arms were not. Poseidon used two of the trident prongs to twist the outer part of the shield backwards, exposing Hades' elbow joint. The kick to Hades' elbow sent the shield flying off his arm.

With his right arm being his one non-wounded limb, Hades had only one move available. Using his right hand to claw into the ground and pull himself, he made like a wounded animal in a desperate attempt to evade

Poseidon. Poseidon glared at him and smiled in satisfaction, knowing victory was near for him.

Hades managed to dodge the strikes at his lower extremities only because Poseidon wasn't making the full effort. Each blow seemed more like he was prodding him to a preferred destination rather than an effort to end the encounter. It soon became obvious why, as the hallway led to a small room with no other ways out. Hades was thus trapped in a corner with nowhere to go.

Poseidon smirked the way Agamemnon did when he laid eyes on the Trojan king, Priam. It was the look of sick satisfaction of a man (or god) who knew he had defeated every countermeasure and could now do whatever he pleased with his enemy. Never being much of a talker, not with Hades anyway, he raised his trident upward to deliver the finishing blow.

Before he could thrust his trident downward for the final attack, he felt a sudden intense, piercing pain in his right shoulder blade. A burning sensation began to travel through him into his right arm. Instinctively, knowing he would have one more attack with that arm, at best, he spun around and hurled the trident at the source of the projectile.

After the trident had left his hand, he saw Athena, Artemis, Apollo, and Hercules at the far end of the hallway. Poseidon snarled in frustration at his cyclops son for not eliminating even one of them. That thought ran through his mind just as Athena caught and deflected the trident with her shield.

The four deities knew they had a small window of opportunity and condensed into a single file line with Athena in the front, using her shield to protect them all. The twins fired off volleys of arrows to each side to keep Poseidon off balance. His arms were damaged, but his legs weren't, even as the burn spread through him.

Poseidon could soon see the whites of their eyes. His four opponents quickly surrounded him, knowing that he now stood no chance of deflecting ALL their attacks. He dropped to one knee and threw a left-hand uppercut into Apollo's genitals, stunning the sun god before he could land a hit from his bow.

Artemis swung her bow into his kneecap, causing him to hunch forward and throw his left forearm upward like a shield to protect his head. Such a defensive move proved futile as Hercules swung his club into

Poseidon's left elbow, rendering it limp and useless. Athena swung her shield like a tennis racket and swatted him into the wall at a high speed. The resulting impact left a man shaped hole in it before he fell back to the floor.

By now, the burning sensation had spread throughout his entire body. Even the slightest attempt to move scorched his insides like the inside of a volcano. The coldest place on earth wouldn't be enough to cool him down. Agony permeated from his head to his toes. Blurry vision overcame him, not quite blinding, but sufficient that he couldn't recognize anyone in the room with him.

Now, the epic five against one mini war had decisively ended. Hades, Poseidon, and Apollo all writhed in agony in separate corners. Artemis, Athena, and Hercules were unwounded but still using the walls like crutches. Even gods could eventually reach exhaustion from such a struggle.

Hades looked at his standing friends with the relief that Penelope felt when she realized Odysseus was finally home from Troy. They looked back him as if to ask if he really thought they wouldn't get there in time. Apollo staggered to his feet and looked at Hades, then his sister. The twins pulled his arms over their shoulders and raised him to his feet.

It was now time for exfiltration. Athena walked in front of them in case Poseidon had called for further help, with Hercules protecting the rear. All knew they would be safe once they got back to the Underworld. Before any of them made it down a fraction of the hallway back to the entrance, Hades dug his feet into the ground.

"Stop, all of you. We're still not finished here."

The rest of the group stared back at Hades in astonishment. What could possibly be left to do after winning a fight worthy of its own epic story? While Poseidon had been thoroughly incapacitated, they had no idea if more of his abominable children were on their way to help him. However, Hades had earned their loyalty, and they looked to him like soldiers awaiting orders.

"Athena, Artemis—I asked if you would help me set things right. Apollo, you're here because you and your sister are a package deal. Hercules, you agreed to assist me as the price for your revenge on Hera. Now it is time for the second phase of this operation. The rest of what we need should be here soon."

Right on cue, the messenger god landed in the entrance way. His winged helmet and sandals were a welcome and familiar site to anyone who hadn't angered the gods. He carried a satchel on his back and was flanked by a thin, blind old man.

"I believe you are in need of my assistance, Hades."

CHAPTER FOURTEEN

RESTORATIVE JUSTICE

"I want to try making things right because picking up the pieces is way better than leaving them the way they are."
—Simone Elkeles, American author

Hades felt his spirit rise at the sight of Hermes and the mortal man. The surge of happiness was sufficient enough to partially accelerate recovery from some of his injuries. He embraced them with the same enthusiasm as a man welcoming his son home from a war. Hermes found it a pleasant surprise—his fellow gods usually took him for granted. The mortal man, however, remained unphased.

"Hades, your plan will change nothing. Olympus will still fall. An invader from a cross."

Athena was now perplexed for the first time ever.

"Across what, Tiresias? They say you see more than those who have sight; share it with us please!"

"A cross, the sea. And the desert."

Hades was now moving like a man sore from exercise, a considerable improvement from recovering from an epic beating.

"Tiresias, I did not summon you here for what you can see but rather what you *can't* see. Hermes, thank you for bringing the necessary supplies."

The rest of the group noticed the satchel Hermes carried on his back

91

and the sack under his arm. All four of them trusted Hades had some sort of plan, but even the goddess of wisdom couldn't fathom what it could be. Each of their glances went to him with a mix of trust and impatience.

"Athena, you are sure that Medusa's corpse is still here?"

"Yes. Perseus only came here for her head—he was a virtuous man. I made sure the headless corpse stayed here. Even I don't know if other parts of her could be weaponized. Her blood spawned poisonous snakes and a flying horse."

"Good, good. All four of you fought well—better than I expected. I wasn't sure we'd be able to overpower him like that. Athena, you outdid yourself strategically."

"It wasn't all me, Hades. Hercules set us up for success long ago."

Everyone turned a surprised look in Hercules' direction.

"Poseidon was incapacitated with one of my arrows. You all knew I dipped them in Hydra blood. What you did not know is that I saved some of them after my Twelve Labors were completed. I buried some near my funeral pyre in case they were ever needed again. I suspected such strong poison could bring down even a god. I'm not all muscle and no brains, you know."

Athena looked at Hercules like her eyes agreed, but her face said, "In your case, I like the muscles better." Hercules looked back like he wasn't thinking about the task at hand anymore. Apollo and Artemis both thought that maybe Aphrodite had snuck in and struck both of those two. Hercules looked at the rest of the group.

"I'm almost as misunderstood as Hades. I also took the less direct approach to 'subdue' Cerberus. He's intelligent enough to make deals, you know. I simply offered him food in exchange for taking a long nap. He found my terms quite agreeable. The part where I wrestled him into submission was an embellishment." Athena now had the same look on her face as Jason when he discovered the Golden Fleece. Suddenly, her dedication to virginity began wavering. Hades knew he would have to play stereotypical father on this one.

"Athena, please guide us to Medusa's remains. We have a more important matter than lust to attend to."

She walked to the front of the group and proceeded down the hallway. After several twists and turns, they came to a room filled with poisonous snakes. This made sense—after all, the blood that fell from Medusa's neck spawned several varieties of them. The blood from her body had therefore spawned more. A cluster of the serpents slithered over a human shaped mass in the middle of the floor.

Apollo stepped away briefly and returned with his bow drawn and launched a flame tipped arrow near the concentration of snakes; it instantly scared them away. No one had to say it out loud. Each of them knew what they had found. Hermes handed Tiresias the small sack he had been carrying. Hades gestured for everyone else to look away.

"We do not know whether us gods are immune to the petrification effect of Medusa's eyes, but now that we've seen Hydra blood stop Poseidon, I'm fairly certain we're not. Hence why I summoned a blind man. Apollo, Artemis, take Athena's shield and bring Poseidon up here. If he resists, knock him out."

Apollo and Artemis complied immediately. While they were gone, Tiresias carefully removed the severed head of Medusa from the sack and set it onto the remains as though reattaching it. Then he folded the sack and placed it over Medusa's eyes like a blindfold. The twins returned carrying a wounded Poseidon on Athena's shield and set him down in the corner.

Hades pulled out a dagger and a cup. He cut a gash into his left arm and held the cup to catch all the blood. Athena, Apollo, Artemis, Hercules, and Hermes all did the same. Tiresias procured a sample from Poseidon. The six of them formed a circle around Medusa and poured the blood samples into her neck.

The divine blood functioned like sutures and reattached Medusa's head to her body. Next, the snakes on her head transformed back into human hair. Her face morphed back into a human one and her tongue shrunk back to normal size. Human legs replaced the snake like tail she had been moving around on.

Each of the god's eyes opened wide. This was a use of their powers none of them had ever thought possible. Hades had let dead men return to the mortal world before, but none had ever attempted to raise the dead. All five of them felt a great chill at the sight in front of them. It felt something like an out of body experience.

Medusa's skin regained the features it had when she was a human woman. Her large black eye circles shrunk and untwisted themselves into human ones. She sprang to her feet, only to immediately collapse back to the floor. It was no surprise her legs were weak—she hadn't used them in years. Her lips began to move, and her mouth began to form awkward words.

"Lleave, nnn-noww. You, you are not, welcome in here!"

Artemis set down her bow and sword to show she meant no harm. She gently offered Medusa a cup, which was reluctantly accepted. The newly revived woman drank the contents and strength return to her legs. Now she could comfortably stand and speak coherently.

"Who are all of you? Why are you here? Why am I here?"

"You don't recognize even me, Medusa?"

The sight of Athena triggered Medusa's old memories. A flash of Athena setting the curse on her. A waking nightmare of Poseidon bending her over the altar in Athena's temple forcing himself on her. One soldier after another crying out in terror before turning into stone. It now occurred to her exactly who she was looking at. Medusa grabbed Athena by her throat and pinned her against the wall.

"YOU! YOU sent me here! I was violated in your house and you banished me to this place!"

Ordinarily, Athena would be able to power her way out of this predicament. This time, she was drained from battling the sea-god and his abominable son. She was also hobbled by guilt. Her wisdom told her that Medusa was rightfully entitled to let out some aggression on her. Artemis gently placed a hand on Medusa's shoulder.

"Medusa, you don't need to do that. We came here to set things right. Please, hear us out." Medusa released her grip and turned to look at the rest of the assembled gods. Hermes handed her the satchel he'd been carrying.

"You probably want some clothes."

Medusa looked down and realized she was naked and cold. Her monstrous biology had made clothing redundant. The prolonged isolation had altered her mind so that nothing had remained human about her. Human intelligence and reason were beginning to reenter her mind. It was no longer instinctive, but she remembered how to dress herself. The satchel contained a fine dress like what had been the uniform of Athena's priestesses.

"Medusa, I am so sorry for what happened to you in my temple. I can't even..."

"What *happened* to me? That's how you describe sexual assault? It happened because you failed to protect me!"

"I couldn't. Not against him. We had to subdue him to get a sample from his blood to help revive you and it took FIVE of us to do it!"

Medusa looked to the corner and saw Poseidon looking like a tiger in a cage: a ferocious beast that couldn't hurt anyone anymore (for the time being). Suddenly, her memory of being violated by him felt less real. Poseidon looked up at her and felt revived. Having his way with her before hadn't quenched his lust and she looked just as appealing now.

"Well, Medusa, I must say you look as *delicious* as ever. I've had many women but you- you were my favorite."

This remark undid Artemis' progress in calming her down. Poseidon's injuries had only begun to heal and even a mortal could damage him now. Medusa seized Hercules' club and pounded the sea god's legs like a slave pounding away at shackles. Poseidon let out screams that caused a tsunami sufficient to douse much of the island.

Being taunted with a reminder of her past trauma had filled Medusa with rage and strength, but she had never been a warrior. It was only a few blows before her arms gave way to fatigue. The exertion drained her enough that she needed a break from standing erect. She sat down in front of the wall. Artemis joined her and put her arm around Medusa's shoulder.

"Medusa, I know you're beyond enraged but try to remember, Athena didn't do it. Poseidon chose to do what he did to you. She couldn't punish him then, but she did now. All of us did. Athena, tell her."

"Medusa, I didn't want to send you here. You were a priestess under an oath of virginity. I never saw what he did to you as *you* breaking your oath. I had to act as I did or he would have come after me. It took five of us to defeat him and that included him being drugged."

"Why this, why here?"

"You were so damaged. I had to remove your humanity to heal you. I turned you into a gorgon to keep you safe."

"Keep me safe? The last memory I have before now is a sword slicing into my neck!"

"I'm the goddess of wisdom, but I'm not infallible. Therefore, my

95

mistakes are the embodiment of foolishness. Your stare had the power of turning people to stone. I couldn't let you petrify innocents, and you didn't want to be around humans anyway. This seemed like the best solution."

"But why did you let them hunt me?"

"Somehow, word got out. Some of them came here in search of glory, others to die. The worst part was the ones who had been sent here by worse men. *They* wanted your head to use as a weapon of mass destruction. A sufficiently evil man could have used you to exterminate all of humanity."

"That doesn't answer my question, Athena."

"Even us gods don't have unlimited power. We never stopped individuals from pursuing their goals before. We still don't interfere with free will. Hades was wondering how he received so many warriors from different nations who were dying one at a time. The efforts to recover the frozen soldiers would have eventually attracted more people here."

"You don't interfere with free will? Shouldn't you be staying out of mortal affairs then? Let men fight their own battles?"

"You sound like Hades. He's been confronting all of us about that lately. I'm literally the embodiment of wisdom so my mistakes are proportionately larger. Yes, I've said that already. I determined it necessary to say again."

"How am I human again?"

"Our blood has the power to revive the dead. We had never tried it before. The five of us were the only gods willing. Just to be sure, we decided to include Poseidon in the mixture. None of us had ever bled before. His blood had to be drawn at the same time as the rest—that's why we fought him here. Not to mention, he richly deserved punishment for what he did."

"So you five did that to him? Thank you, Athena. If gods and powerful men faced consequences like this then they might think twice."

Hades saw this statement as his cue to interject in the conversation.

"We had to do this quite carefully. Confronting him in the Underworld could possibly have allowed the dead to escape. I recently allowed a single dead man back into the world of the living. His presence nearly triggered a storm. We'd rather not find out what would happen if that were multiplied."

The rest of the group's eyes opened wide at the thought of whatever could have happened. Athena had of course planned out the fight. Hades had arranged for the absence of certain other Olympians. Hades saw everyone was *still* exhausted from the encounter. It seemed a good idea to further establish *why* they did it this way.

"If any more of us had been here, we could have created an extinction level event for humanity. I sent Charon out to sea to warn all the nearby ships back to port. Sailors will enjoy much smoother journeys while Poseidon recovers. The only reason he couldn't destroy us immediately was the concoction Dionysus made for him. Oh, by the way, be careful with him. If anyone asks him to, he'll be happy to help drug any of you."

Medusa replied, "I'd prefer to have nothing to do with him or any of you for a while. I appreciate the rescue, but it was a god who made it necessary in the first place."

"I won't bother offering you your old position then." said Athena.

"I have a new position in mind for you." Poseidon said with a smirk.

The twins raised their arrows to fire before Hades raised his hand to stop them. He picked up Athena's shield from the ground and smashed it into Poseidon's lower abdominal/genital region several times. Such blows would end any mortal man's bloodline forever. Finally, he kicked his head into the wall behind him to render him unconscious.

"Hermes, deliver him to Tartarus. It won't hold him for long but perhaps it will teach him some manners. Although, if the beatings we just gave him didn't get through to him, nothing will."

Hermes grabbed Poseidon by the hair and flew away with him. This had the unexpected effect of rejuvenating the drained deities. Medusa felt as though she had now witnessed everything she wanted to see happen to her assailant all those years ago. Now it occurred to her that she was going to be leaving her island of exile.

"I don't know where to go now. I never considered anywhere other than the temple."

"How would you like to regain your ability to defend yourself, retain your humanity, all without having to live in isolation?" asked Artemis.

"I would love that. What did you have in mind?"

"There's an all-female tribe of warriors out there called Amazons. Most of them were born into it and they have an aversion to men. They don't normally accept new members, but they happen to be devout followers—of me. Would you like for me to introduce you to them?"

"By all means yes."

A horse was heard braying in the distance. Instinctively, the remaining group headed in that direction and stepped outside the temple. They were greeted by the sight of a majestic white horse with vast beautiful wings protruding from just behind its neck. Its facial expression said it was beholden to no one but chose to be of service to those it felt worthy.

Artemis jumped onto his back with the grace and ease of a seasoned cavalry soldier. She smiled at Medusa and held out her hand. Medusa took it and Artemis smoothly pulled her up and backward behind her. Their flying mount rocked backward in response. Medusa reflexively wrapped her arms around Artemis and much to her surprise, felt safe for the first time in as long as she could remember.

"Pegasus is a smoother ride than you would think. Don't worry, he'll get us there."

The former priestess felt a mix of surprise, gratitude, anticipation, nerves, and hope. For a second, she considered swearing an oath to Artemis as she had Athena. Everything about the goddess of the hunt said she would never victimize or neglect Medusa. For the first time in her life, Medusa was in the company of someone she could trust, and for now, that was enough.

CHAPTER FIFTEEN

THE IMPEACHMENT OF PARIS

"A gentleman accepts the responsibility of his actions
and bears the burden of their consequences."
—William Faulkner, American author

H ades sat in his chair with considerable difficulty remaining upright, for he was still recovering from his brawl with Poseidon. His legs and back ached, as though crying out for him to be nowhere other than in bed. He had been told that the few mortals who ever reached old age felt this a way at a minimum every time they woke up in the morning. For the first time ever, he envied mortals as they had death to free them from pain.

Persephone entered and placed her hands on his shoulders. She didn't mind being the doting and dutiful wife some-times as Hades had never demanded it of her. He didn't treat her like it was her divinely ordained destiny imposed on her just for being a woman. It surprised her that Hades could be damaged by anything physical. She had accepted that his heart was as vulnerable as any mans, after the Trojan War wore him down over the years.

"I didn't think anything was ever a risk for you gods, Hades."

"Only when we confront each other, my dear."

"You had to do it carefully, didn't you? Is this why Zeus is in a similar position, only from drinking and not fighting?"

"Yes. If he and Poseidon and I ever fought all at once, it would likely destroy all of humanity. I had to prevent him from getting involved."

"Why not just ask him?"

"As the mortals say, 'it is easier to ask for forgiveness than permission.' Oh, I could have persuaded him to stay out of it, but there would still be a risk of him changing his mind. Fortunately, he accepted the challenge offered him."

"What challenge?"

"From Dionysus and Hermes. I simply visited Dionysus. We had a few drinks. He challenged *me* to a drinking competition. I told him I enjoyed drinking with him casually, but Zeus would probably be up for it. Then I asked for something to drug Poseidon with. I told him I thought it would be funny for Poseidon to wake up hungover on a beach. And that he should add in something that would impair his strength. That part was necessary too—if he were at full strength, even five of us wouldn't have had a chance."

"Now it makes sense what I've heard from Olympus."

"Why, what have you heard?"

"Hermes told me that Athena and Hercules haven't been seen in a while. They were last seen entering his room. Even Aphrodite couldn't believe what she heard."

"What rumor did she hear?"

"Not rumor—noise coming from Hercules' room."

"I only stopped them from going at it in Medusa's lair because we had a task at hand. The two of them and the twins fought Poseidon with me. After Athena learned Hercules had intellect to go with his strength, that was it."

"What was the task at hand?"

"We brought Medusa back to life."

"You did what?" Persephone asked, stunned.

"I will fully explain that one at a later time, Persephone. I shall wait until Zeus is recovered from his hangover to meet with him. In the meantime, I still have a mortal or two to deal with. Could you please bring Prince Paris in here?"

Persephone smiled at him and walked away. Hades dug into the arms of his chair to steady himself. The anger he was already feeling toward Paris was close to making his blood boil and his legs were shaking. He calmed himself to avoid letting out the kind of anger that could destroy part of his domain. The worst possible thing that could ever happen under him would be the dead escaping. Persephone returned with Paris, looking at him with an expression that said she was glad not to be in his position.

"Prince Paris of Troy. Do you have any idea why I summoned you here?"

"No. I don't know what I did to piss you off."

"Has the sheer number of your fellow Trojans that joined you here escaped your notice? I imagine it has. I've never known you to care about anything other than yourself."

"You've never known me at all."

"No, but I know the results of your actions."

"What are you talking about?"

"Your hormones ignited a major war," Hades said this with the cold fury of a man who knew his anger was bubbling towards the surface.

"Yes, but wasn't the war inevitable anyway?"

Hades stepped towards him as if to ask Paris if that was really the answer he wanted to go with. Some of the arrogance and obliviousness slipped off the prince's face. Hades clenched his fist tight enough for his fingernails to draw blood from his hand. The sound of his natural breathing was scarcely distinguishable from the snarling of a wolf.

"Don't tell me you wouldn't trigger a war to tap that. Didn't you abduct your wife anyway?"

Hades threw a left-hand punch into Paris' throat and a right-hand strike into his ribcage. The same blow on a living man would have simultaneously cut off blood and oxygen flow to his brain and shattered most of his rib cage. The dead still physically moved and spoke like the living but without the usual functions. As he had with Agamemnon, Hades had restored enough of Paris' life functions to enable him to feel pain again.

"Perhaps I shouldn't punish you to the extent I had in mind. I'm not sure it would be right to punish someone as foolish as you. You must be a fool to insult someone as powerful as I."

"How is it an insult to state a fact?" Paris asked naively.

"I sometimes forget that the story of how Persephone and I met has been twisted and falsified."

"So, she was in on it, just like Helen."

"I didn't trigger a war doing it!"

"Yes, but didn't her mother withhold the harvest until she was returned? *You* nearly caused the extinction of humanity!"

This statement burrowed into Hades' heart. Of course, Persephone had had to pretend to be kidnapped by him to get away from her mother Demeter, but they never anticipated she would react *that* badly. Regardless of the intent or anticipated results, they had still set in motion events that endangered all of the human race. Hades then thought that maybe the destruction of one country wasn't nearly as severe.

"Us be damned, you are correct, Paris. I never considered how my actions effected innocent people either. I was ready to inflict the most brutal punishment I could think of on you. Now, I realize I might be equally guilty."

Hades felt the strength leave his legs as he stumbled backward into his throne. Most of him went numb from the shock to his system. Of course, he and Persephone didn't have the same knowledge of the likely consequences of their actions as Paris and Helen did, but they still made a calculated decision to do what they did. Hades had at least tried to set right the problems his fellow gods created. By sheer luck, no one had died from the problems created indirectly by *him*.

"I see now that you may not be as guilty as I originally thought, Paris. Yes, it was your decision to abscond with Helen. They still had the option not to do what they did. My fellow gods made a habit of disproportionate retribution well before Menelaus or Agamemnon. Your failure of guest friendship should have been considered an offense by *you* against Menelaus himself. It is an unfortunate habit of rulers to comingle their personal identity with that of their nation. Had Menelaus found a way to kill only you, and done so, I would consider him a good man. Perhaps emotion overruled logic with everyone. However, emotion completely replaced by logic is also undesirable. Paris, is it true that you and Menelaus faced each other in battle?"

"Yes. He easily defeated me. I survived only by the grace of Aphrodite."

"Aphrodite. How appropriate. It was her bribe that got the whole ball of death rolling. Menelaus felt that a great many people in a distant land had to die because of his wife's infidelity. A man like him could easily find another wife!"

"As you said, he comingled his personal identity with his country's."

"Yes, as though everyone, from the next in line for the throne down to the lowliest peasant, was *personally* harmed. I'll bet he genuinely thought *every single subject* of his would rather die than let their king be embarrassed. Yes, the abduction of Helen ground life in Sparta to a halt. Years from now, people will tell their grandchildren how they instantly dropped everything else to defend the honor of their ruler!"

"My father said the war was inevitable anyway."

"Yes, Priam and Aphrodite each said that as well. How honorable of her. It was your acceptance of her bribe that brought you and Helen together. Tell me though, did you consider the other offers?"

"How would that have been any better?"

"Athena offered you wisdom and skill in war. Hera offered to make you King of Europe and Asia. Why did those things appeal to you less?"

"All three of them also got naked. I wanted to tell which ever one I picked that I'd accept her offer if she herself was part of it." Paris answered.

"Paris, the results of you thinking with your hormones are the reasons I was inclined to lock you in the Brazen Bull and forget the key. You are Influencing me back towards that idea."

"Well, I think Hera's offer probably would have caused problems too. Making me King of Europe *and* Asia—how many rulers would *that* piss off? Troy probably would have had more than just the Greek armies at the gate."

"I'll grant you that one. Perhaps you do have a functioning brain after all. Hera was punished for her part in that dispute—that and the multiple homicides she was responsible for."

"*She* fought in the Trojan War?"

"Hera intervened, but I was referring to what she did to Hercules. The blood stain that set into my table there came from Hera's *head*."

"You mean, gods can bleed?"

"Only when we attack each other. It's not quite the same as it is for humans. We can't die but we can be damaged and feel pain. That hole in my wall happened when Hercules kicked Hera into it."

"It sounds like that bitch deserved it."

"Watch your tone, Prince Paris. Remember, I can hurt you worse than any Greek ever could. You wouldn't have death to end the pain if I did."

"My apologies, my lord."

"Alright, I can accept why you would resist Hera's offer. Why Athena?"

"I was a healthy, virile young man. Wisdom wasn't something I was interested in. As for the skill in war, why bother? Hector did a rather good job of that."

"Athena in her wisdom should have figured that out." Hades agreed.

"What exactly do you plan to do with her?"

"Athena has answered for her actions. She was more repentant than you. Or most of the gods for that matter. Now that I think about, if you had accepted skill in war, you might have turned Troy into an invading and conquering power. Now I see why accepting the 'most beautiful woman in the world' appeared the least destructive option."

"So, no punishment then?"

"I didn't say that. You haven't been as smug and arrogant as I expected. I wonder, did you consider the problem with accepting Aphrodite's offer?"

"I *was* worried about the wrath of the other two."

"A valid fear, but no. Aphrodite offered to give you another human being. Did that strike you as wrong in *any way*?" Hades questioned.

"People buy and sell human beings all the time."

"And what makes *giving one away* any better?"

"It's just what people do. The people with power anyway."

"I will not punish you for your acceptance of human trafficking, but *only* because none of you humans have ever had the idea that it's wrong. When Aphrodite made the offer, did you stop to consider what it might do to the woman in question? Did you think Aphrodite was carrying Helen in a sack, ready to hand her over immediately?"

"I did... not consider that. I thought only of my own desires."

"I'm surprised you're able to admit that."

"I've had time to think about it. Humans can recognize the error of their ways even after they get here to the Underworld."

"Very few of them recognize it *before*. With every other confrontation, I have been sure of what to do with them immediately. In your case, I am in doubt. *For the time being,* I will not make your afterlife any worse than it already is. The contest you settled—I still have to confront Zeus. *He* failed to stop it when he had the chance. And failed to protect the innocent from its consequences."

"Do you mind if I leave now before I get in more trouble?"

"Yes, return to your shuffling around aimlessly. Persephone!" Hades waved him away.

Paris made a cautious exit from the throne room. Persephone passed him on her way back in, surprised to see Paris still able to walk. It was also a pleasant surprise to her that Hades did not appear any angrier than when he sent her to bring in the next defendant. She sat down in his lap and stroked his hair. He didn't wince in pain at the weight of her.

"Hades, you're calmer than I thought you'd be. I thought he'd be screaming until his vocal cords were torn to shreds."

"I had initially planned to make him suffer. He threw it back at me."

"How?" she asked.

"We set in motion horrible events just like he did. I know we didn't expect your mother would withhold the harvest until you were returned but we still set that ball rolling. It's one of the few times Zeus ever put his foot down with any of us."

"I'd arrange my own kidnapping again if I had to do it all over. And I'm happy to be with you. You've proven to be so much better than just a means of escape, Hades." Persephone kissed him to add emphasis.

"Paris still helped cause the fall of Troy. *We* nearly caused the end of humanity."

"It was my mother's decision to react the way she did, not ours."

"That is true, just as it was Menelaus and Agamemnon's decisions to react as they did. The biggest disproportionate retribution in human history. I've already confronted Hera, Athena, and Aphrodite. Zeus could have stopped the madness. He will be my next confrontation."

"You should do it soon. Poseidon is still recovering from the five of you. Still, if Zeus reacts badly, the two of you could destroy Olympus—at a minimum."

"I'll have Dionysus slip him some of the same potion he gave Poseidon, only without rendering him unconscious. Just enough that he can't fight at full strength. That way he'll be pretty agreeable to discussing things in a civilized manner."

"Or you could invite him here. You have the strength advantage in the Underworld."

"That sounds like the most sensible option. How do I get him here though?"

"I think I know a way..." she said mischievously.

"Tell me more..."

CHAPTER SIXTEEN

ZEUS

"The greater the power, the more dangerous the abuse."
-Edmund Burke, Irish statesman,
economist, and philosopher

Zeus, the god of thunder and ruler of the sky. The King of the Olympians, great victor of the Titan War. As he walked into the Underworld, he wasn't thinking about living up to any of these things. His thoughts were more inline with his title of, well, a nickname hasn't been assigned. It was said he sired enough illegitimate children to raise an army. He was also said to be a serial rapist, but that hadn't been discussed—until now.

Regardless of his past deeds, Cerberus perked up at the sight of him. He was sometimes as misunderstood as his master but that didn't get to him. For him, anyone coming in other than the newly arrived dead were friendly visitors. All three of his tongues stuck out of their mouths and all his eyes went wide. He was disappointed as Zeus strode by without an acknowledgment and let out a whimper.

Zeus stopped in his tracks. He believed Hades didn't know he was here, and the guard dog might alert him otherwise. The only thing to do was walk up to Cerberus, scratch him behind his ears, and tell him what a good boy he was. This had the desired effect: Cerberus smiled and relaxed himself back into a contented sleep.

Now there was nothing in his way. The thunder god made his way into Hades' throne room with a swagger no god or man could match. His reason for coming was lounging on the table: Persephone. Zeus took one look at her and almost began to drool on the floor. He'd had his share of beautiful women, but his brother's wife still impressed him.

"Persephone, I see your time down here hasn't dulled your beauty. There's something quite alluring about the dark look."

Persephone stood up off the table and walked up to him, running her fingers over his shoulders and chest. Zeus knew she would, no woman could resist him, mortal or otherwise. Oh yes, that divine magnetism never failed him before and it wasn't going to start now. No matter how many times he experienced it, the feeling was still exhilarating.

"You look even better in person, god of thunder. How would you like to try something new?"

"What do you have in mind, fair maiden?"

"Fisting."

"I've never heard of that particular act. What does it involve?"

Persephone shot him a satisfied smile right before he received his answer. The right side of his jaw felt like it had been hit by a battering ram. His body rotated ninety degrees and he fell face first into the floor. Blood flowed freely from his nose and mouth. His eyes widened as he saw his brother Hades standing over him.

"Hello, brother. It's *so good to see you again.*"

"Hades? What is the meaning of this?"

"You have a lot of nerve asking me that question after coming down here for a dalliance with my *wife.*"

"She invited me!"

Persephone fired him an indignant look.

"You *really* didn't find anything suspicious about that, Zeus? You've never visited down here and then suddenly Hermes showed up and told you I wanted to do you on the table in here. You can't believe any woman would ever not be interested in you, can you? Good god, your power is matched only by your arrogance! I believe my part in this is done." Persephone said before walking away.

"Persephone, you're welcome to stay. I value your input."

"I'd prefer to keep the floor in here clean. Your brother makes me sick."

"This was a deception?" Zeus asked incredulously as Persephone made a hasty and enthusiastic exit.

"Yes, brother, it was. We need to talk."

"Why didn't you just come to Olympus? Contrary to what you may think, you're still welcome up there."

"Because that's where you're strongest and if anything went wrong, an outburst from you could possibly kill many mortals. And you're already responsible for quite a bit of that."

"And how is that Hades?" Zeus prodded.

"A little something called the Trojan War."

"Ah, yes, that nasty business. I think that's why I kept getting more prayers for a while."

"You really do get around, don't you? You think about fornication so much you can't even remember the biggest event in our history?"

"*Of course I do,* brother. I do believe it was the first time all of us had gotten involved in something since… we overthrew father."

"And the rest of us did appreciate being liberated from his stomach. He had a horrible diet—it was nastier in there than you could imagine. But that doesn't excuse your behavior since."

"What behavior would that be?" Zeus said innocently.

"Your misdeeds could fill an entire library on their own, Zeus, but let's start with your more recent actions. You did do a decent thing near the end of the war when you made Achilles return Hector's corpse for burial. Other than that, you did nothing but meddle the whole time."

"All of us did. That's kind of what we do."

"No, that is *exactly* what the *rest of you* do. I didn't intervene in the Trojan War, not a single time. For me, every possible outcome would have been the same. Everyone involved would eventually come to me whether the war occurred or not, whether the Greeks or Trojans were victorious. Of course, most of you didn't let the war happen: *you did.*"

"Me? How was any of it *my* fault?" Zeus asked incredulously.

"You didn't exactly order either side to instigate it, but you failed to prevent it. Do you remember a certain contest between Hera, Aphrodite, and Athena?"

"I don't pay much attention to what my wife does but I think it involved a golden apple."

"That's the biggest understatement you've ever made—but we'll cover that in due time. *She* certainly paid attention to what *you* have done. You conscripted Paris to settle that little feud by selecting a winner."

"Ah yes, I remember now. He accepted Aphrodite's offer, which turned out to be Helen of Troy. The face that launched a thousand ships. I'd have nailed her myself if I hadn't been so busy with the war."

"All three of the offers carried the risk of great disaster if he had accepted them. You were *right there* when they made the offers. You couldn't think up a single alternative?"

"I figured it would continue anyway afterwards. Hera and Athena would probably scheme to acquire the apple anyway. My daughter might embody wisdom but she's still a little prone to foolishness. As a bonus, it would keep my wife distracted from my *other* pursuits."

"I'm glad you brought those up. Your 'other pursuits' led to at least three murders—and those are just the ones I can recall right this minute. Would you care to hazard a guess at what I'm talking about? Here's a hint: It's the reason your wife has been recovering from major injuries ever since Persephone invited her down here. Or tell me, did you not mind that because it benefitted you for everyone to think *you* beat Hera to a bloody pulp?"

"She's always been a jealous bitch."

"I'm talking about Hercules."

"Oh yes, I promoted him to full god status after his death."

"I must thank you for that. That's how he was able to be quite an asset when we confronted Poseidon. Haven't you wondered why you haven't seen *him* in a while?"

"Hercules was powerful enough to incapacitate both Hera *and* Poseidon? Why, this is my proudest moment as a father!"

"Hera yes, Poseidon, no. It took *five of us* to defeat Poseidon. Hercules joined us as the price for me letting him destroy Hera."

"Five of you—who? And why did you confront Poseidon?"

"That is not important right now. What does matter is *why* Hercules wanted to do what he did. That hole in my wall, the dent in my table and the blood stains all over the floor all came from her facing consequences for her actions, which were the results of *your* actions."

"Speak plainly, Hades; you're talking in circles."

"Hercules exists because you couldn't keep it in your pants. Hera didn't take it very well and decided to take her rage out on him since she couldn't take it out on *you*. She drove him to insanity and he murdered his wife and two children. You did nothing to protect him. Or them."

"We might intervene in mortal affairs, but we still allow them free will," Zeus argued.

"Us be damned, Zeus; it was still caused by WHAT YOU DID! You acted recklessly with no regard for the consequences for anyone else! Do you have anything to say for yourself on this one?"

"I'm the King of the gods. I can do what I want."

"I think you need an ethics lesson, brother."

Zeus became puzzled at this assertion. What exactly did Hades intend to teach him? In the next few seconds, he got an answer in the form of a massive blow to the spine, sending him flying into the wall near where Hercules had kicked Hera before. Hercules felt great satisfaction at informing his absentee father of his displeasure.

"Hello, *father*. I appreciated being promoted to god, but that doesn't make up for years of neglect." Zeus responded by hurling a lightning bolt into Hercules' chest. It had roughly the same effect as a taser on a 300-pound man high on PCP. Lightning bolts had never failed him before; it was a scary new experience for him.

"What, how—I didn't make you *that* powerful!"

"Brother, you should know that all powers besides mine are reduced down here. It's a precaution we set up so we'd all be safe from each other in our own domains. Also, I managed to give Dionysus the idea to challenge you to that drinking contest. He knew he'd need to use some extra potent stuff to beat you. As Hera also found out the hard way, I can enhance the strength of anyone I choose when they visit. Hercules, I don't think he understands—you haven't been clear with him. Why don't you elaborate a bit? The lesson will end as soon as he demonstrates comprehension of the material."

Hercules approached Zeus and lifted him by the throat with one hand. Remembering that his fellow gods couldn't be choked to death, he hurled him into the opposite wall. After allowing him to get back to his feet, Hercules landed a swift kick to Zeus' groin area. The thunder god reacted much as any mortal man would at the impact. Before his mind could fully process the pain, his face was introduced to the wall several times. Hades looked on with grim approval.

"Well, brother, at least now you won't be able to produce any more children you won't be caring for. For a little while, at least. Now, if you're ready to listen, I can instruct your teacher to end today's lesson early."

Zeus nodded in agreement and Hercules left the room. Hades brought Zeus a goblet to drink from. Zeus reluctantly accepted it and it dulled the pain. At least, enough of the pain for him to think and speak coherently. His legs were undamaged, so he was able to make it to a chair and seat himself.

"Now, Zeus, I do believe we've covered the Trojan War and Hercules. What shall we cover next? Oh yes, I recall that you and Poseidon exterminated all but two humans. I think you used a great flood, didn't you?"

"The humans of that time did worse things than we ever did. They sacrificed each other to gain our favor, at the drop of a hat! I've heard reports of how much the people sent here by the Trojan War upset you so much but why didn't you confront us back then?"

"I did, brother. It's been a long time. I brought it to your attention, and you did something about it. I think it must have enraged you as much as it did me." Hades answered.

"It did. Poseidon didn't need much persuasion to help me with the flood."

"Now that I think about it, I think I know why your intervention helped there and did not during the most recent war. You and Poseidon acted with no interference from the rest of us. It had the intended effect of giving humanity a restart," Hades explained.

"Yes, so did Hera. Letting her do what she wanted created the force that would have killed me right here in this room if I were capable of death."

"Zeus, YOU created that force. Then Hera's reaction set him in motion. You promoted him into the pantheon out of guilt, didn't you?"

"Yes, yes I did. I felt it was also a justified reward. Hercules had suffered a tragedy and trauma worse than any human ever did. He could have placed all the blame on Hera, but he did not. Humans that do terrible things seldom have remorse or make any effort for atonement. Most of them justify it."

"Hercules must have knocked the arrogance out of you." Zeus said.

"More like he forced me to admit what I had always tried to deny."

"And what would that be?"

"That no matter what our intentions, our actions bring devastation and pain." Hades said.

Zeus's face suddenly became cold and pale. All his memories of everything he had ever done came flooding back. He became overwhelmed with trauma. For so long, he had used his power to think up new ways to gratify his sexual urges. As he processed the accusations of Hades and the strikes of Hercules, the ripple effects of all the god's actions ran through his mind.

"Brother, I think we've reflected enough on our past mistakes. We should examine now how to proceed forward." Hades declared.

"Agreed. We're both here now. Let's get Poseidon in here. We should go about this as we did when we divided the spoils after overthrowing our father."

"Our brother is still recovering from my previous confrontation with him. We had best do it carefully. I needed the help of Athena, Apollo, Artemis, and Hercules last time. Victory was only possible because he had been drugged. I could have fought him here but the damage might have enabled the dead to escape. If you, Poseidon, and I all fight each other, it will likely eliminate all of humanity."

"We could have Hermes bring him to Olympus before he fully recovers. That way, he won't be inclined to try and fight the two of us."

"That might work. The three of us should discuss the situation amongst ourselves first then, summon the rest. Zeus, I don't know if a practical solution to the problem can be found. The greatest threat to humanity other than themselves is us. How do we protect them from both?" Hades questioned.

"I don't know, brother, but we will find a way, or a way will find us."

CHAPTER SEVENTEEN

GATHERING OF THE GODS

"It was through Pride that the devil became the devil: Pride leads to every other vice: it is the complete anti-God state of mind."

-C.S. Lewis, British author and theologian

Hades and Zeus sat in their great seats in the circle of twelve on Mount Olympus, where the pantheon met whenever necessary. Each seat was decorated with imagery and symbols appropriate to its occupant. Hephaestus had crafted all twelve from marble and enchanted them to contain magic and power that would reduce anyone else to ash immediately on contact. From these chairs, they had ruled over the fate of humanity for eons.

Zeus' great throne was sky blue and adorned with two gold encrusted eagles that lit up brighter than the sun when touched by him, and the back rest had an engraved image of a lightning bolt. Hades occupied a shiny black marble one, emblazoned with many smaller images: his beloved wife Persephone, his guard dog Cerberus, Charon and his boat.

The two gods did not have to wait too long for their brother, not that time was of any concern to them. Poseidon arrived with the aide of the messenger god Hermes, mostly recovered but still limping. His condition had improved from a wounded soldier at death's door to that of an athlete sore after a sporting contest. He waved his hand to rearrange the chairs so the three of them could face each other.

Poseidon sat in a chair made of fine marble, colored the dark blue pattern of the sea. It was decorated with appropriate marine iconography: a trident on the back rest, sea horses, massive waves, sirens, ships, Scylla and Charybdis. It felt warm and cozy like a heated blanket yet still kept him upright and alert. He looked upon his two siblings with surprise and familiarity.

"Be warned, Hades—I'm nearly fully recovered. I haven't forgotten our last encounter."

"I was hoping you wouldn't. The point was to teach you a lesson."

"Oh really? Not just to get a blood sample from me?"

"Why did you take his blood, Hades?" Zeus interjected, surprised he hadn't been informed of this beforehand.

"To do what we should all be doing, Zeus—set right that which we have made wrong."

"And which wrong were you righting?"

"You might recall how he forced himself on Medusa in Athena's temple. Athena ended up banishing Medusa to an island lair. Dionysus and Apollo figured out that Medusa could be restored to life with a sufficient mix of our blood. Six were needed. Poseidon's had to be one of them, so the five of us beat it out of them."

"I had heard of sparks between Athena and Hercules. I'm surprised I can't hear them going at it right now. Is that how they came together?"

"Yes, they developed a battle forged attraction from that endeavor. We're not here to discuss only the two of them, however. All of us have sins to atone for. Even me."

Poseidon looked at Hades with great surprise. He had never known his brother to interact much with anyone—fellow gods, mortals, etc. The only interactions he knew Hades to have were his wife Persephone, guard dog Cerberus, and underling Charon. Hades was known not to interfere with mortal affairs as they would all end up with him anyway. He would now have to elaborate.

"It is widely believed I abducted my wife Persephone. That is partially true. She wanted to be with me, but her mother Demeter would never let her go. We staged her kidnapping so she could come to the Underworld.

We never expected she would withhold the harvest and thus use all humanity as a hostage until she was returned. You ordered me to return her, Zeus. The only way we could stay together was for her to eat food of the Underworld and tether her there. I never imagined Demeter would threaten to kill humanity by starvation."

"How was her reaction your fault?" asked Poseidon.

"I set it in motion. No matter what their intentions, who ever sets in motion a chain events, bears part of the blame for that which follows. Poseidon, do you understand how what you did to Medusa could have gone far beyond that?"

"No..." Poseidon replied with a tone lacking the arrogance he had spoken with before and indicating he didn't know the answer but acknowledged it was something he must face.

"Athena told me all of it when I called her out. Medusa was reduced to an empty shell after you violated her. Athena did the one thing she could protect her: turn her into the Gorgon monster, complete with the ability to turn people to stone. Ares told her how grave an error this was: Medusa's severed head could have been used as weapon of mass destruction. Fortunately, Hermes and Ares mitigated the damage that was done." Hades explained.

"Will you be granting her the power to exact revenge on me like you did for Hercules with Hera?"

"No. She already did. After we resurrected her and made her human again, she broke both your legs with Hercules' club. It appears the beating and subsequent time in Tartarus impaired your memory."

Poseidon sat in silence and pondered over the revelations he had absorbed. His eyes went open wide as though a conscience had bit into him like a poisonous snake. After all, the guilt now burned him inside like venom would. His body felt heavy all over and most of it began to sweat.

"I, I can't believe...I could have set in motion the extinction of Humanity." Poseidon gaped.

"I don't believe you could have foreseen that but, you should have easily thought of the effect it would have on *one* human."

"Medusa."

"Yes. I've met women like her when they arrive in the Underworld. Not priestesses of Athena, but rather ones who were violated like she was. Many were killed right after enduring that trauma. Every dead soul eventually goes cold, numb, and blank, still retaining memory and speech but otherwise not human. The ones who arrived like Medusa though—they were like that already. Now that I think about it, they were one of *my* sins as well."

"How were you responsible for *them*?" asked Zeus.

"I didn't harm them, of course, but I have failed to help them. I will no longer let the men who did that to them live out eternity in the same place as them. They must be made to pay for what they did. The Trojan War made me realize how cruel it is that so many mortals suffer and die for the actions of distant rulers they'll never even meet. I think the very least I can do in the Underworld is isolate the oppressed from their oppressors. A system where they are judged based on their actions in life would be best. Since this will affect all of us, I will bring it to the whole pantheon before I enact it." Hades finished.

"Poseidon, Hades is quite right. And the distant rulers who cause them to suffer include you—and I. Our continued interference in the affairs of mortal men brings about mostly disaster. We can't continue like this, brother," Zeus advised.

"I must agree, Zeus. Shall we summon the rest?" Poseidon agreed.

"Hermes, bring them all in," Hades commanded.

Athena and Hercules appeared almost instantly. They had heard his voice as they were at Olympus anyway. The two approached Athena's chair and realized there was a problem: too small. Hercules sat down and pulled Athena onto his lap. She liked the marble chair decorated with carvings of olive trees, owls, a helmet and spear even better now.

Ares walked in with the demeanor of a soldier facing a battle he knew he likely wouldn't return from. He had a quiet focus, unlike the fiery rage normally associated with him. The chair he sat in was still exactly what one would expect for the god of war: blood red, crossed swords on the back rest, arm rests shaped like spears, a comfortable and functional monument to battle.

Hera arrived, walking like an athlete waking up the morning after an epic contest. The bruises and scars from her previous meeting with Hercules had nearly faded away. She rested herself in a grey chair encrusted with a stone pomegranate, cow, lion, peacock, and scenes of marriage and childbirth. The usual disdain for Zeus remained, but even she knew he wouldn't call such a meeting unless it were of great importance.

Apollo and Artemis came in and sat in adjacent seats. Both were fully recovered from the showdown with Poseidon earlier, most likely due to Apollo being a god of medicine. His throne was bright gold like the sun, featuring iconography such as poetry scrolls, apothecary supplies, and a harp. The silver arrow shaped arm rests were the one deviation from the gold sun color motif.

Artemis sat in a beautiful moss green seat, reflective of the woodlands she preferred to spend her time in. A bow and quiver adorned the backrest. The rest showed pictures of a stag, the future temple that would be built in her honor, and the sacrifice of Iphigenia. After her previous meeting with Hades, she had had the sacrifice scene added to remind her not to do such things again.

Hephaestus walked in with his usual limp. His expression bore the resigned look of someone chronically underappreciated. Long had he been the one the other Olympians consulted when they needed something. After all, his designs had never once failed them. He would have had much more enthusiasm to craft things if they showed any interest in *him*. The craftsman god seated himself in a solid, simple metal throne bearing images like a forge and anvil.

Aphrodite trudged her way into her sphere of the circle with the air of an aging beauty queen. Not that she had aged like a mortal woman per se, but with a face bearing the weight of painful self-reflection. Guilt had eaten away at her like acid on a wall ever since she realized what she did with Helen. She sat in her soft red throne depicting scenes of sex and romance, roses, waterfowls, and swans like a criminal defendant in a court room.

A sound of grunting and exertion echoed all through Mount Olympus. The assembled Olympians weren't quite sure of the cause until Hermes entered the room doing an over the shoulder carry of the wine god Dionysus. The god of the vine, wine making, ritual madness, ecstasy, and theater was larger and fatter than any mortal man to ever live at the time. Were he not a god, the extra weight would surely have crushed his knees. Zeus looked on with resigned contempt.

"Dionysus, it now seems quite cruel of me to send *Hermes* to fetch you up here. A cargo of *your* weight calls more for the strength of Ares, or even Hercules!"

Dionysus wriggled around on his chair like a house cat, looking for exactly the right spot to be comfortable. It was wider than the others to accommodate his girth, painted a bright purple, and embellished with images of grapes, wine goblets, a pinecone tipped staff and satyrs with fully erect penises. After finding his comfort spot, it dawned on him where he was and possible reasons why.

"Zeus, why did you bring me up here? I was trying to sleep off a party. This is kind of cool though—I never expected to wake up here. It's a lot nicer than the places I usually wake up. And some how I have all my clothes on."

Hermes looked over at him with a mild irritation. The messenger god sat in a chair emblazoned with the caduceus staff, feet carved in the shape of winged sandals and the magic satchel he used to deliver whatever divine objects necessary. His body felt a great rush of relief after the exertion of conveying Dionysus to the meeting. Zeus looked at the now fully assembled Pantheon to proceed with the unpleasant purpose of the summit.

"Thank you all for coming. We are gathered here today to address the cumulative results of our involvement in the affairs of mortals. I must give Hades the credit for this one, I don't think any of us would have reflected on it if not for his intervention. I will let him have the floor."

"Thank you, Zeus. We have been interfering with the affairs of mortals for too long. Even our best intentions have piled up bodies as high as mountains. With the possible exceptions of Dionysus, Hermes, and Hephaestus all of us have blood on our hands that we can never wash off. If you don't believe me, just ask any of the Trojans now in my custody. Either way, we need to ask ourselves where we should go from here. What do you think?"

The rest of the Olympians looked around nervously at each other. All seemed to have a great many thoughts, questions, suggestion and comments running through their minds. They squirmed in discomfort and their heartbeats accelerated. Hermes felt it the worst—his palms were sweaty, his heart burned like Troy at the end of the war, and he was now lightheaded. There was only way to relieve himself of these symptoms.

"You are wrong about me, Hades. I have blood on my hands like the rest of you. I've just been better about keeping it hidden. I can't pretend I'm clean any longer," Hermes declared.

The pantheon gasped in astonishment. The other eleven gods had never seen Hermes as lesser than them per se, but, also never though him as powerful or influential either. Their messenger always struck them as being gentle with mortals, never delivering wrath of his own but merely relaying theirs. Each of them began to formulate in their minds what sort of misdeeds he might have committed. They didn't have to wait long for an answer.

"Her name was Apemosyne, daughter of the King of Crete. Her brother, Althaemenes, found out about a prophecy that one of them would kill their father. They fled to Rhodes. I saw her there and became overwhelmed with lust. I forced myself on her. Althaemenes didn't believe her when she told him. He kicked her to death."

This revelation had the same impact as the news of Helen fleeing Sparta. Even after honest examination of themselves and each other, they still believed him incapable of the same misconduct as them. Hermes had always been a dependable messenger, spending most of his time away from supervision. Either way, he enjoyed the same lack of accountability as the rest. After it sank, in he continued.

"I also raped a water nymph named Lara. And I met her only because she informed Hera of one of Zeus' affairs and he cut her tongue out and sent me to take her to the Underworld. She couldn't even scream. The end result was twin sons." Aphrodite decided to try and comfort him.

"Hermes, most of us have multiple illegitimate children. Including me, which were also sired by you. Ok, there's no way around this; we've all been terrible. I'm in a polyamorous marriage with two of you which only became necessary because of my chronic adultery. I'm sorry, Hephaestus," Aphrodite said.

"Aphrodite, there is no need to apologize. You're enough of a handful that no one man or god can handle you alone," Hephaestus tried to joke.

"I was always happy to send you home afterwards," replied Ares.

Hades knew he had to get things back on track.

"Ok, everyone, this supposed to be a *strategy* meeting, not group therapy. However, it does seem to be a secondary benefit. This only underscores my statement that we've all been reprehensible. The best thing to come out of this summit so far has been multiple rape confessions. I'm thinking of changing how we handle the mortals after death."

"*We?* Don't you mean—*you?*" said Hera, as the rest nodded in agreement.

"The only mortals who face any punishment are the ones who have pissed off someone in this room. Men like Sisyphus and Atlas, and I'm not sure they deserve the eternal agony we've imposed on them."

"Go on, Hades. What alternative do you propose? If Atlas doesn't hold up the sky on his shoulders, who will?" asked Apollo.

"I think we should transfer that task to different offenders from time to time. Agamemnon did more to deserve that fate than Atlas did. All he did was fight against us. Agamemnon, on the other hand, set soldiers against women and children. He burned Troy just to satisfy his greed," Hades reasoned.

Ares rose from his seat. "I've never told this to any of you except Hades. I have a window into the mind of every man who has ever fought in battle. I see the torments of the Greek soldiers who survived that war. I share their nightmares where they remember the things they did, saw, heard, and smelled. Agamemnon was already a wealthy and powerful king before all of that. He still used the flight of his brother's wife as an excuse and sent men who had nothing to fight, bleed, kill, and die so he and others like him could have *more*. His wife killed him for sacrificing their daughter to get to Troy, but I think he got an easier and quicker death than he deserved. Hades has him in the Brazen Bull. I think he should replace Atlas in his duty for a while. After him, butchers like Alexander should have a turn. Does anyone object?" Ares asked.

As Ares sat down, Artemis stood up.

"You said you would have that burden transfer from one offender to the next. Hades, Ares, what would you do with Agamemnon after someone replaces him?" Artemis questioned.

Hades replied after a short pause.

"I think Tartarus would be appropriate. We have reserved it for only the very worst so far and I think he qualifies. All in favor of that plan of action?"

Everyone present raised their hand in support and a feeling of relief permeated the room. This was their first collective effort to undo the damage from all their interference. They reached a bit of a dead end though, for while punishing the mortal who did the most to push the Trojan War was important, it wasn't nearly enough. The Olympians all sat in silence for a long while, for no one had any idea where to go from there.

FINAL CHAPTER

OLYMPIAN TWILIGHT

"Old soldiers never die- they just fade away"
- Douglas MacArthur, General of the Army

The once grand home of the gods now held an atmosphere of despair and impending death. Its once glimmering thrones occupied by the deities now resembled long neglected constructs of mortals. Guilt and regret from their occupants had seeped into the foundations like invasive species. Where they had once come to rule as deities, they now congregated like lowly mortals in a dingy tavern.

Nervousness about the future was soon replaced by fears of the present as an unknown individual entered. None of the Olympians knew what to make of him. His clothes were dazzling white but otherwise, he could blend into any mortal crowd. He carried a shepherd's staff and stood at average height with brownish skin tone, and a beard, like a man who had spent most of his life in the desert yet had not suffered the ravages of such a climate.

Reactions from the pantheon were varied. Hades had a look of resignation as though the inevitable had arrived. Zeus and Poseidon wondered how he would dare enter their sacred space. Hera thought he might be a jealous husband seeking revenge on any given one of the men in her life. Aphrodite thought he was striking—in a primitive sort of way.

Athena recognized that it would be futile to try and prevent him entering, a thought that did not occur to her twin siblings.

The sequence that followed happened almost too rapidly for even gods to perceive. Artemis and Apollo rose from their seats of power as though accepting a fight challenge and fired several shots from their bows as though the stranger was an invading army. The dozens of arrows may as well have been pebbles as he caught them with both hands and snapped them with minimal effort. The twins gave each other a familiar look and charged their deceptively formidable opponent.

The stranger proved to be as proficient with his staff as Poseidon with his trident or Zeus with his lightning bolt and landed blows that briefly turned them mortal. Ares' hand went to a sword on his hip as Athena held up hers to stop him. His sister's wisdom had never steered *him* wrong before and he refrained from attempting violence. Even Zeus gripped his throne chair tightly to try and hide the shaking in his legs. Hades rose calmly and approached the stranger as he would any arrival in *his* realm.

"Who are you? Why are you here?"

"I have many names. Feel free to use any you like, Son of God, savior of humanity, Prince of Peace—yes, I know that's ironic considering what I just did to two of you, Yeshua, King of the Jews—you probably haven't heard of them. Most commonly, I am known as Jesus Christ. To put it bluntly, I'm here to discuss a 'regime change'."

Eleven of the twelve Olympians all reacted the same way they last did when Hera proposed over throwing Zeus. The patriarch produced a lightning bolt and gave Christ a similar look to the one he had given Cronos many years ago. His family was now united in a way that they had not been since the overthrow of their predecessors the Titans. As tenuous as their rule over mortals was, they intended to defend it as zealously as the Trojans defended Troy.

"How dare you enter the home of the gods and speak such insolence! The other eleven of us *combined* were not enough to overcome me! I was able to make them labor for centuries, building the walls of Troy—what do you think all *twelve* of us can do to you?" asked Zeus.

"Oh, I rather think I will accomplish more with the aid of twelve *mortals* than you will with your twelve gods, thunder man. Look at your palace. It is beginning to fall apart, is it not? Have you any idea why?" Jesus asked.

"We are presently divided, yes, but we have quarreled before."

"Are you sure? Have you not felt your followers drifting away?"

Zeus put away his lightning bolt. Ten of the twelve Olympians shared a look as though a nightmare had come to life. They *had* heard of a new faith entering their territories, but they thought it had merely been a fringe belief system with a very persistent marketing department. They had heard whispers of a man called Jesus but were under the impression that he was merely the invention of some creative minstrels. Reality had now entered their mist and they knew they were powerless to stop it.

Hades and Dionysus were the two who didn't look terrified. Dionysus's face lit up like a child meeting their favorite costumed character. He rose from his seat with the renewed vigor he usually felt when his hangovers wore off. Suddenly, he was able to move with the same swiftness as Hermes and made his way to give their visitor a warmer welcome.

"I've heard about you! You're that guy who can turn water to wine! Please—join me for my next party!"

Christ looked at him with the amused but distant acceptance of someone interacting with an eccentric relative. It shouldn't have surprised him that the god of *wine* would greet him with such enthusiasm. He knew later that he would have to explain that other than an enthusiasm for wine, the two didn't have much in common. His next move would have to be to keep the meeting on track.

"Thank you, Dionysus. I might take you up on that. I see it's dawning on the rest of you—your strength is tied to the beliefs of your followers. As they pray to you less, you feel more. You are still immortal yet some of you are beginning to feel the pains of mortality that come with old age. When humans begin to live longer, they will learn to age gracefully—I suggest you do the same."

Athena maintained her usual poise and bearing but could not hide her confusion, a great pain for the literal embodiment of wisdom. She looked at him with a curiosity she hadn't even felt back when she first sprang from her father's forehead. This situation, however, presented a challenge akin to getting past Troy's great walls. The only approach here though, was to be direct.

"How have you managed to undermine us so? You have neither command of the sea nor control of the sky nor the combat prowess..." Athena asked.

"I think Artemis and Apollo would beg to differ on that last point, Athena. This staff is not even designed to be a weapon, yet I used it as you would a sword. Your worshippers are not drawn to me for any martial prowess or raw power. No. I am far more appealing to them. For example, Lord Hades—how are the dead handled under *your* charge?"

"For much of history, equally. The Trojan War inspired me to change things a bit. After my wife showed me a broken child who was killed *after* the war, I realized I could not continue that way."

"You had only been punishing or rewarding the absolute best and very worst of humanity in the Underworld. Under *me* though, salvation is available to the *common* man. And I would rather not discuss how you have handled them while they walk among the living..."

"We have recently changed that policy. One of the worst mortal offenders will now have to hold up the sky for eternity."

The rest of the pantheon nodded in agreement as they had already been called to answer for their action involving the mortals. For most, it had been the only visit they had ever made to the Underworld. While they had recognized their sins amongst themselves, it was still galling to them to hear this visitor mention it to them. Hera could not silence herself any longer.

"Yes, we committed a few indiscretions among our mortal charges, but what makes *you* any better?"

"Well, I will admit I was a bit of a disturbance to some of them. A few money changers lost a bit of money. I'm sure none of you would have tolerated that behavior either though. At least I haven't provoked any sort of massive war."

This retort enraged Ares as much as the lack of temples named for him did. His mind seemed to briefly channel Athena as he decided to engage Christ in a different form of battle: debate.

"Hermes, bring in the Fates! We have received visions and images of the future, *Prince of Peace*! If you have never provoked war then explain why *your* name will be evoked on the field of battle one day!"

As Ares finished his tirade, Hermes reentered the throne room with three ragged looking women. They had the demeanor and affect of deaf mutes but could cause fear among even the gods without speaking a word. Their visions of the future had once guided the gods to victory but recently brought about fear and confusion. They projected a series of visions onto the nearest wall. "In the name of JESUS CHRIST! "shouted a knight with a large red cross adorning his chest, before plunging a large sword into an unfortunate soul on foot.

Poseidon chimed in, "If that's not enough for you, let's get to the actions of your future recruiters!"

"At last, Christianity has arrived in the new world," the future explorer Columbus was shown recording this entry into a journal he wrote in from the inside of a newly built church, as his underlings chopped limbs off natives who failed to provide adequate gold.

"Shall we continue?" Poseidon asked.

"To be fair, I'll never *tell* anyone to do such things. At least *four* of you directly escalated the greatest war your followers ever fought. I'm looking in your direction, Athena, Aphrodite, Hera, *and* Artemis. And Apollo, *you* guaranteed the death of any non-combatants who might have survived. Hades was right—you cursed all of Troy when you retaliated against Cassandra."

The Olympians pondered over Christ's words and realized that he wasn't wrong. None of them could think of a single incident of him taking side in any of humanities armed conflicts.

"My name will be invoked on many battlefields in the millennia to come. Soldiers nervous for battle and wounded ones who will soon meet me in person. My father and I will ignore most of them- After all, their enemies will often ask me for help too. I will, however, occasionally aid individuals. Ares, would you like to assist us?"

"No. I don't even want to continue. I'd rather you simply put an end to me."

Christ gave him the look of someone having to break the news of a loved one's death and put his hand on Ares' shoulder.

"Ares, you are the embodiment of war. Even *I* am not powerful enough to end war itself. There is some good news for you. As soldiers begin to pray to me instead of you, you will lose your connection to them. You won't have to share their memories or nightmares anymore. Now, you know how war is those who have much sending those who have nothing to kill and die so they can have even more."

"I certainly do," Ares replied.

"I will send you to aid the occasional soldier in battle. You will guide otherwise non-violent men in combat. There will be many of them who my father will have a plan for where they must survive through their war. Ares, the deeds they commit driven by you will be recorded in their history books. You will help them do things where they will be decorated for valor."

"And how exactly is your approach any better than ours, you glorified carpenter?" interjected Poseidon.

Christ replied, "Said the rapist. Oh yes, my representatives will one day commit crimes like yours—against children, no less. I won't intervene to stop these priests but unlike *you*, Athena, I won't turn them into hideous beasts who are hunted by the followers of Ares."

The Olympians viewed him with a mix of rage and the feeling that he was right. Most of them had intervened in the affairs of mortal men more times than anyone could ever know. As the guilt began to sink in, the visitor continued.

"My followers know I will eventually return. I haven't decided when, except that I might change the date should any of them successfully predict it. I could easily directly intervene anywhere I want. When men kill on my behalf, I can easily appear and tell them no, I don't want you to do this, but it would be as you people say, opening Pandora's box."

Everyone present looked at him with astonishment that he knew the story, and that he would reference it in front of them.

"Oh yes, make no mistake, your influence and names will live on in history. Artemis and Zeus will have monuments listed as two of humanities greatest achievements. Aphrodite, your name will be a synonym for sexual desire. Ares and Apollo, your names will one day be associated with space travel. And *all* of you will be depicted in many works of popular fiction— not as many as *me* but still a respectable number."

Eleven of the twelve Olympians looked at each other, all knowing what they were thinking, none wanting to say it out loud. Zeus knew as the leader of the pantheon it was his duty to do so.

"Very well. Greece is yours. Our fractured rule has led to fatherless children, childless parents, blood-soaked beaches, and cities ablaze. We will step aside. Remember however that we cannot be killed. As you said, our names will live on."

Hades stepped forward.

"There is but one condition, Christ. Even where we, or you do *not* intervene, much of mankind is subjected to domination by their fellow man as though we were stepping on him. I would like to build a portal at the entrance to whatever you make the afterlife."

"And where will it lead?"

"To an alternate version of the time they spent on Earth. A parallel world where Troy is still standing because the men involved found a way to solve the problem without a full-scale war. A world where they are not swept away by war, famine, or disease like dirt in a storm. A mortal lifetime where they will reach their full life expectancy. Not one free of struggle but one where they live each day without paying for the bad choices made by distant men they'll never even meet."

"Very well. I will provide them in the afterlife with the life they could never have. Either way, they will then proceed to one based on their own conduct."

Christ walked to the balcony and watched the sun rise over the horizon. Apollo realized one day humanity would no longer believe that to be *his* handiwork. Hera, Athena, and Artemis thought of all the women who would still suffer in the eons to come. Ares realized that man's inhumanity to man would likely keep him around eternally. It dawned on Poseidon how much of Earth could one day have been his domain. All twelve realized they could never die, but the time had come for them to fade away.

ABOUT THE AUTHOR

Anthony J. Miano is a former soldier and current broadcaster. His Military Occupational Specialties include 19D, Cavalry Scout and 37F Psychological Operations Specialist. Mr. Miano is a graduate of the University of Akron and the Ohio Media School. He also cohosts the NoOutletLive podcast. A lifelong Akron, OH resident, he enjoys trivia contests and dogs in his free time.

Printed in the United States
by Baker & Taylor Publisher Services